TWO ONCE THERE

By

Jeffrey Curry

FOREWORD

Two Once There continues the story of *Two Once Removed* where Callie Larson and Jason Cartwright cross paths a second time after their impromptu weekend of rediscovery ten months earlier. Although reflection and backfilling are included to remember key points from their weekend, *Two Once Removed* should be read first to ensure a complete understanding of this shared journey.

The *Two Once* series are self-published books editted by avid, volunteer readers, not professional editors. Therefore, some minor writing issues may still remain in this story.

1

Callie watched the July heat ripple off from the pavement as she drove behind the oceanfront homes and cottages. Without thought, her right hand reached up to push the button to open her sunroof while her left waited to do the same to lower all four windows of her Range Rover. The resulting exchange of the cool air-conditioned air with the heat, humidity and smells of the North Carolina ocean worked their magic to release the tension that was building inside of her. After fifty-one years of life and twenty-six years of marriage, she now felt that she was back where she needed to be.

The wash of warmth and the sunshine over her fit body resulted in unwanted perspiration that quickly dried as her body adapted to its new environment. After pushing her blowing chestnut brown hair back from her tan face, she reached over to give a quick pat to her five-year-old Cocker Spaniel, Molly, who was always at her side. Up until that point, Molly was settled in a curled position on the passenger seat as she typically did on road trips. But the jostling of the warmer air and new smells made her curious to sit-up to look out the window.

For different reasons, both Callie and Molly were excited to be back at the beach. For Molly it was a newly found place of freedom to run with a companion who suited her. For Callie, it was where life blew-up ten months earlier after making sense just moments before. As time passed and her marriage imploded, Callie ran countless mental run-throughs on how this return would play. As she pushed her hair back a second time to rest behind her ear, she began to feel anxiousness return as she sought to find out what remained for her down the street after her abrupt departure in October that had no follow-up until now.

The final quarter mile of her trip was filled with thoughts that drifted back to the day her life of kids, husband and family all changed. Just prior to then, that time was supposed to be exploding with parental independence and opportunity to live again. At fifty years of age, the time of life that everyone said was so wonderful while she was still young, healthy, and wealthy enough to enjoy it all with her husband, had finally arrived. But to her surprise, her empty nest freedom became isolation as her kids bounded off to college and her husband continued to choose his heavy business travel over her.

What was supposed to be the ideal set-up that included all the resources to do whatever she and her husband wanted to do turned dark. And like water turning off from a spigot, Callie immediately found herself alone and isolated in their large Washington DC area home she used to covet when it was filled with the life and activity of kids who were now gone.

As she approached the driveway of the small, non-descript cottage that became her touchstone of hope in the fall, Callie was happy to see it received a desperately needed new cover of gray paint. It was simple improvement that would have given her a far better curbside first impression last fall. But regardless of whether it had been painted or not when she first saw it, she knew she would have turned her nose up at the little, beach-front box had she been seeking a vacation rental for her kids and husband.

Underneath the cottage was the parking pad she remembered that included the usual lines of posts that supported the cottage above it. Callie's heart nervously started pounding as she saw his familiar older Jeep Wrangler parked in its usual spot by the stairs that led up to the living area and views. Beside the Jeep, she was surprised to see an unfamiliar, older Volkswagen Rabbit sitting in the shaded spot she used last fall. The make and age of the car told her it likely belonged to one of Jason's daughters. One she had not met given that the only one she did meet drove a Mini Cooper convertible that was much newer and nicer. Reality and nervousness were now hitting her stomach as she gently pulled her Range Rover onto the packed gravel pad to park behind the Wrangler. She paused to think as she watched the sunroof glass slide shut. She then simultaneously pulled the window buttons two at a time to close her car from the elements.

Callie could hear her breathing become louder as she clipped Molly's leash onto her collar. As the driver door opened, Molly hopped over the center console to follow her mother eager to see if Jason's Chesapeake Bay Retriever, Zoe, was home to greet them. Callie's movement was deliberate as she closed the car door and walked slowly toward the stairs while studying the familiar surroundings. Molly, however, had a different desire to get moving. She was eager to search and pulled Callie to go find Jason and Zoe.

The added Volkswagen was intriguing and added to her nervousness. When she noticed a small VT logo on the rear glass, her anxiety increased with it confirming she was about to meet the second of Jason's four adult daughters. Callie immediately placed VT with *Virginia Tech* which meant Jason's second youngest daughter, Faith, along with possible friends, maybe even a boyfriend, was visiting. Callie remembered from their conversation last fall that Jason's "Virginia Tech" daughter was studying neuroscience with a dream to go to medical school. The 'brain studying the brain', as he put it.

The thought of another one of Jason's daughters, and her friends, being at the cottage for her unannounced, *surprise return*, added to her angst. She already had significant doubt on whether making this visit as a *surprise,* after almost ten months of total silence, was still a great idea. But their agreement was clear when she left with her husband in October. Callie had to work everything out at home, alone, with her husband and family, before she could reunite with Jason in any way.

The two days Jason and Callie spent together the previous October that unearthed revelations and temptations not pursued, was not planned. Prior then, the two had not spoken in twenty-seven years. Their last words then happened not long after Callie broke off their engagement five weeks before the wedding day. Her reason was that Jason was struggling, distant, and seemed to be fading away. Callie discovered that Jason was divorced, retired, and living at the beach when their mutual friend, Sandy Worth, showed her a Facebook post he had posted. It was a general invitation to friends to visit. It was a post he positioned to find Callie.

Heading into summer, Callie questioned whether the feelings she rekindled with Jason in the fall were either real or caused by her loneliness. She also wondered if they had survived the ten months of silence she needed to figure her life out. Meeting another one of his daughters, particularly the smart one, added to her already stressful return. When a bead of perspiration finally broke loose from her brow down to run down across her cheek, she realized that she was delaying her arrival by standing frozen in the driveway heat staring into space.

As Callie returned to conscious thought, it occurred to her that she had the same opportunity to chicken-out just as she did in October. The purpose of that trip was to answer curiosity. The two-hour drive from Williamsburg was just to check him out from afar. But when a chance sighting of Jason at a gas station gave her opportunity to see him then let him go, she ran to stop his car as he headed to the exit. Her need to see him then was the same as it was now. And like before, it pushed aside all the hesitations that were popping up in front of her.

The Jeep parked under the cottage was Jason's daily driver. It was a newer model of the same type of Jeep he drove when he dated Callie and when they were engaged. She ran her hand across the driver's side as she walked by. The weekend they had in October was hosted, in part, by that Jeep as they drove from place to place with the top down to enjoy the salt air, stars and moonlight. That Jeep, along with his small, then dilapidated, old beach cottage, was her renewed impression of him. A *romantic* image that stuck even though she knew he had raised four daughters, built, and sold a company, and was in a position to retire at the age of fifty-five.

As Callie began to walk into the shade under the cottage, she surveyed the area for life. Muffled music from above along with a loud thud told her someone was home. As Molly continued to pull her forward to the familiar stairs that led up to the cottage, the views, and the walkway to the beach, Callie pushed through her final resistance and took her first steps to go find Jason.

# # # #

The sounds of the surf and screeching seagulls grew louder as she strolled past the side, windowless door to reach the back deck that faced the water. A quick look through the sliding glass doors that faced the water did not reveal anyone inside the cottage. As she turned to search the beach, it was just as she remembered. The only change from October were far more families huddled in chairs with tents placed in front of their respective homes. Swimmers were out enjoying the waves. Her internal pull toward the sand and the water was subtle but strong enough to keep her moving toward the bench at the top of the stairs.

As she lightly glossed her hand lightly over the bench where she and Jason came back together in October, she looked out beyond the surf hoping spot him again taking a swim, just as she did in the morning last fall. But instead of seeing him freestyling with his modified flippers and trailing lifesaving bullet, she noticed the chairs they used in October set near the waterline occupied by several young adult bodies consumed in books and masked by their chair backs and baseball hats.

Molly's excitement to see the beach was immediate recalling the fun she had in October with Jason's retriever Zoe. With the gate down to the sand open, Molly made an immediate dash to down the stairs until the limit of her leash stopped her. After several more scans, neither Jason nor Zoe were anywhere to be seen. None of the readers in his chairs appeared to have his build.

"Can I help you?" startled her.

The voice was young and female. As Callie turned to reply, Molly bolted back up the stairs to greet the person who had just inquired from behind. The leash slacked then pulled again causing Callie to lunge forward. As she stumbled and regained her footing, she looked to greet the tall, early twenties woman with flowy blond hair who was looking back at her.

"Hi," was all Callie could only muster as Molly's yank and the stumble exhausted her air.

She took another pause to pull herself back together and to clear her face of the hair that fell forward during her stumble. When she was finally able to get a good look, she saw a warm, welcoming smile of a college-age girl who was now on her knee petting Molly. The sight itself relaxed her. The girl in front of her had to be Jason's daughter Faith.

On her visit in October, Callie got to know each of Jason's girls through his stories and descriptions. Callie's snoops on Jason's Facebook over the years provided her with a familiarity with each of them as they grew from adolescence to young adults. She knew what each looked like before seeing Jason again. But, just like seeing him in October for the first time in twenty-seven years, Callie's impression from screenshot to real flesh was going to change dramatically. Stunned, and not knowing what to say, she just stood quietly gazing.

"I know who you are!" Faith declared in a surprised tone. "You're the one in the picture with my dad that's on the counter."

Callie gave a puzzled look to the comment. She did not recall any pictures being taken of them during her fall visit. A photo of her from almost thirty years ago would look dramatically different. It certainly would not be an image Faith would easily apply to her now.

"But my dad refused to tell us who you are," Faith added. "But we think Maya knows."

Callie smiled recalling her time with Maya. As Jason's youngest daughter, Maya showed considerable spunk and maturity during the few hours they shared when she arrived unexpectedly during Callie's surprise visit last fall. In that brief time, it was clear to Callie that Maya and Jason had a special connection, an alliance, that Callie found common to the one she had with both her parents. Maya would hold any secret Jason asked her to.

"It's Callie," she replied. "I'm not sure what picture you're referring to."

"I'm Faith… Daughter number three," Faith answered with some humor. "The picture is a really nice sunset shot of you and my dad from last fall. I think Rebecca took it."

Callie's expression showed amusement as her thoughts quickly ran back through the fall weekend and time spent with and near Jason's emergency room doctor friend, Rebecca. She specifically remembered being afraid and making a special effort to not be in a position where any pictures taken with Jason could look improper, if discovered. She left Jason thinking she had been successful in that effort. But, in hindsight, she knew that every phone, in every pocket, at the happy hours they attended, had a camera.

Callie's thoughts quickly changed back to the moment as she started to wonder if she would even like the picture. Being caught with him by her husband, Chase, in October ended the worry that a photo would surprisingly appear on social media to cause strife to her marriage. But Jason's past choices of picking pictures of her were sketchy at best. She had hope that *their friend* Rebecca would have better taste and only have given him one where Callie looked extraordinarily good.

"It must have been from one of the happy hours," Callie answered.

Faith smiled knowing the reference. Callie's tone showed that she was not as careful as she thought. The parties hosted by the usually closed group of original family cottage owners, called the *Abbie's,* were legendary. Short for 'Aborigines', Maya talked about some of the parties she attended when the four sisters were together for Thanksgiving and again with their mother for Christmas. Despite the fact that Jason had only owned his cottage for one summer season, stories from those happy hours were abundant, funny, and rivaled some college revelry the girls' thought was unique to their age group. Faith found most of it hard to believe until she experienced one firsthand this summer.

"I'm sure it was," Faith replied, amused with thoughts of phones pointed at Callie and her dad. "Too many people with cameras."

Callie continued to hold her smile as she ran through her weekend with Jason last fall. It was bugging her as she remembered her fear about photos of her with Jason finding their way back online to Washington, D.C. Although they were caught by her husband Chase just as she was about to leave the cottage, Callie still worried about the impression and embarrassment a sordid affair, that didn't happen, would harm back home for her, her husband and, most of all, her three children.

"Is your dad here?" Callie asked.

Faith's face sank with the question. In the excitement to meet the woman in the picture, she completely forgot that Callie was there to see her dad.

"I'm sorry. He's gone," she answered stoically.

Callie's stomach sank as she heard Faith's answer. She noticed that Jason had stopped posting on his Facebook after she left his cottage in October. She assumed it was to help her by not throwing anything out there that would affect her process of working through her family and marital problems. As he declared during her visit, it was vital that he *not be a speck of consideration* in her marital workout. So, it did not surprise her when periodic checks on his public Facebook page showed nothing new.

To live-up to their agreement and to make the most difficult decision in her life, Callie also adhered to the no contact promise. The one exception was a single text she sent him on Thanksgiving Day when the usual bliss of the holiday and family she loved blew up in front of everyone. Her text was short and simple. It asked him *to wait* for her. It was a text he was waiting for, coveted, and did not reply to.

After that one unanswered touch, Callie went completely dark to anything *Jason.* She knew she needed clarity and focus to clearly work through her life for what it was and what she wanted it to be. Her internal conflicts of kids, family, faith, and marriage were concrete and amplified by both empty nest loneliness and Jason's life, availability, and confessed love for her as *his one.* In his words, it was a love that started on the day they first met over thirty years ago and never ceased. A love that was completely obliterated by Jason's self-destructive personality at the time.

"I didn't know," Callie replied shocked and tearful to the news. "How?"

Hearing the news hurt. It was something she should have heard from their common friends from childhood or, at least, from his daughter Maya. He did not appear sick when they were together. Her face drained of color as she turned and looked off into the distance.

"Oh, no," Faith blurted out with laughter. "He's not dead. He's just not here. He's in Asheville... up in the mountains until to-morrow."

Callie's sorrow did not allow her to immediately process Faith's clarification. Her blank expression held for a few more moments until the updated news sank in. As it did, she exhaled heavily as her shoulders raised higher and a smile of relief lit her face.

"I'm so sorry," Faith added while still giggling.

Callie saw Faith's amusement as an extension of Jason. He would have found the misunderstanding funny too. Her stomach and thoughts, while still reeling a bit, all began to trend back to calm with the news.

Asheville was a place he never mentioned to her. It was, how-ever, familiar to her from a family trip she took with Chase and their three kids a few years ago. Their trip was educational to see the famous Biltmore Estate. It was a family spring break vacation that faced heavy resistance from everyone until they arrived, toured the exquisite property, then experienced the artsy life and food of Asheville. Asheville was on Callie's empty-nest travel list to visit again with Chase. But, without the kids.

The news that Jason was doing something in Asheville did not surprise Callie. He had an inquisitive, artsy side that would align well with the community that was there. She knew his casual disposition would fit in there just as it did on the Carolina coast. Callie also found it nice that his girls were now visiting him at the beach which meant that, at least for the time being, both the cottage and he were going to continue to be in close proximity to her mom's home in Williamsburg.

"Your dad wasn't expecting me," Callie offered as she pondered her options. "I just thought I'd pop in for a surprise visit."

Faith did not know what to either say or offer the woman who was obviously a strong interest to her dad. Their short encoun-ter made her want to talk to Callie longer to learn more about her. Her fit, polished, casual look was something Faith knew her dad would dig. So, she decided it would be fun to invite her to stay to enjoy the surroundings as well as for her and her sisters to dig in deeper. It was killing her to want to see what potential the woman in the picture, who showed out of nowhere, had to offer. The worst that could happen was that she would say "no".

"You're welcome to join us," Faith added quickly not wanting to let the opportunity pass. "It's just Maya, me and Rachel. The guys are just friends from school that are staying elsewhere."

Callie felt a nervousness bind her stomach as Faith finished her offer. Three of his daughters were there. And he was not. Some of the edginess of the daughters without dad was a little removed because Callie already knew Maya. She also found Faith was to be warm and friendly.

The drive back to her mom's was an easy two hours. So, Callie knew she could go back there and return either tomorrow or the next day when she knew Jason would be home. Callie needed more time to think. It presented an interesting opportunity for her to talk with Jason's girls without him being there. That revelation offered a unique and attractive opening to learn more about him. She did love her brief, somewhat anxious, talk with his youngest daughter Maya in the fall. A talk that started on the shaky ground of misunderstanding but ended with a hug when Maya cleared-out to give her dad the space he needed to be with her. From Faith's comments, it appeared that Maya never shared any of that experience with her sisters.

With all the potential of being able to ask his girls questions, Callie also knew it would also be their chance to probe her for information. Details that both he and she may not want to share. The overall intrigue was building to be too much to refuse. But after thinking through it all, she felt that being safe, at this point, was worth more than the information she could uncover.

"That's very nice of you to offer," Callie answered. "I think I'll just head back to Williamsburg and try again to catch-up with your dad when I'm back in the area."

Faith's face showed immediate disappointment. Selfishly, she wanted to know more about the woman in the picture. But her reasons to leave were easy to see. Williamsburg was not that far away. Faith passed it every time she commuted down from Virginia Tech. So, she knew Callie was not going to disappear into the darkness if not held in place now.

"Ok," Faith answered. "I'll let him know you stopped by and were looking for him."

Callie nodded agreement as she started to move then stopped.

"No," she said abruptly. "I want this to be a surprise. Please don't tell him I was here."

That statement amplified Faith's curiosity to know more about the woman in front of her. She could see that Callie was determined to get out of their awkward parental love-interest / daughter conversation. With a slight frown to try to guilt her to hang around, Faith yielded a path for Callie and Molly to make their way back to her car and escape.

# # # #

Driving behind the row of oceanfront homes with the convertible top down, Maya was fighting off the swirl of her hair as she downshifted her Mini Cooper to prepare its final approach to the parking pad at the cottage. Usually, she sported a baseball cap to ponytail her hair away when driving her Mini topless. But, in her haste to get to the store, she was already on her way when the first real blow of air made her realize she left her hat on the kitchen counter. The drive was not far. So, going back to the house for just a hat was not worth the effort.

As Maya approached the cottage, her angle and abrupt reduc-

14

tion in speed shifted the packages on her front seat forward. Her peripheral vision saw them slide and pulled her focus from the upcoming driveway to the bags that were headed toward her passenger seat floor. Autopilot quickly took over to help guide the car through its final approach onto the driveway as she reached to grab the bags that were teetering to fall.

At first, Maya did not see Callie's black Range Rover. From the road, it was partially blocked by the neighbor's cars as its black color blended into the shaded background of the bigger homes sitting behind it. When the Range Rover did appear in sight, Maya quickly swerved to avoid a collision. The action resulted an odd parking awkward angle on pad with one of the Mini's front tires in the sand. After taking a moment to collect herself from the excitement, Maya looked back at the Range Rover wondering why her mother would be visiting her dad. It was more than a year after their amicably tumultuous divorce settled. As far as she knew, there was nothing more for them to discuss.

The Black Range Rover was always in discussion with Jason's four daughters. It was their mother's first purchase from the proceeds of her divorce settlement with Jason. The mothership HSE, with its dark, tinted windows, looked ominous. And, although Maya's mother loved the beach, visiting her dad's cottage, even with him away, was not something that seemed like it should be happening.

As Maya realigned her car back into the slot next to the Range Rover, she noticed the same white Virginia license plates that perplexed her last fall when she made a surprise visit to the cottage for Columbus Day weekend. Although confusing then, this time it was clear who was there. Callie was back. And, hopefully for reasons different from last fall when her visit ended in a fight Maya feared could happen between her dad and Callie's husband Chase.

The fight was won by her Jason without much effort. More importantly, it was won without either striking or hurting Chase. An awkward sucker punch by Chase, that missed, threw him off-balance enabling Jason to push, pin, and bury his face into the sand next to the Faith's current parking spot. But even though Jason won the fight, he would later admit that he lost the battle. After heated words between the three, Callie left with her husband to go back to Washington to work out their family and marital problems. A step Jason told Callie earlier she had to take even if it meant she stayed with Chase.

Maya's heart began to pound as she raised the convertible top. Her impression of Callie was that Callie was her dad's *ONE*. That term was Jason's to represent the *ONE* each person is meant to be with.

As Maya set the windshield roof-locks in place, she pulled up on the toggle switches to close the windows that sealed her car from the elements. She then quickly checked herself in the mirror to fix her hair before grabbing the bags full of fresh shrimp, Margarita mix, and other items she had purchased at the local shoppes. Maya was both excited and afraid to see Callie again.

As she headed for the stairs, Maya heard two voices from above grow louder. One she recognized as Faith who was doing most of the talking. Faith was training to be a doctor; so, asking questions was already embedded, and growing more dominant, in her DNA. Maya smiled when she heard the second voice. Not because she had heard it many times before, or even recently, she knew from the black Range Rover with the white Virginia plates that the voice conversing with her sister Faith was Callie's. As she started up the rustic wood stairs to the cottage, Maya's breathing began to labor as excitement and anxiety grew within her.

Callie appeared at the top of the stairs first still engaged and looking back as she finished her comment. Molly stood patiently at Callie's side until she saw Maya. Her excitement to see Maya made her instinctively run to greet her. As the lease reached its limit, it again pulled Callie off balance causing her to stumble down the stairs.

Callie let go of the leash to catch herself on the wood handrail as she twisted to regain balance and to stop. As she recovered from the excitement, she looked to find Maya a step below her with her bag-laden arms out to catch her. Maya's eyes were wide open in anticipation. As they calmed to the excitement, smiles and laughter of relief soon replaced the panic on their faces. The thrill to meet again made them forget about the bad result that was just avoided.

"I knew it," Faith declared as she watched the two regain their footing. "I knew you knew who she was."

Maya reached to touch Callie to ensure she was stable and OK. She then looked toward her sister with an expression to demand compassion for what just happened. Callie straightened her jostled shirt as she worked to pull herself back together again.

"Dad asked me not to tell," Maya directed at Faith in a firm tone.

"Since when do you do anything either of them ask you to?"

Callie was amused by the question. As the third of three daughters, she never hesitated to share particularly saucy or embarrassing parent news with her sisters.

"Faith! Just shut up!" Maya answered as she turned to Callie. "Are you OK?"

"Fine," Callie answered, still checking her clothing. "Not quite the entrance I wanted to make here or how I thought I'd meet any of your sisters."

"It's all good," Maya reassured her with a smile. "We've all tumbled down these stairs. So, you're in good company."

Callie laughed as she began to feel a burn on her forearm. As she lifted it to look, she and Maya noticed a dollar-size abrasion that was beginning to bleed. Callie's face showed embarrassment as she looked toward Maya.

"That looks pretty unfriendly," Maya stated sarcastically. "Let's get *doc* to look at that. My guess is it'll make her queasy."

Callie relished Maya's jab at her sister. It reminded her of her own relationships with her two sisters. Both she and Maya were kindred spirits sharing the challenges and privileges that came with being the youngest in a house of girls. Callie turned as Maya and Molly passed her on the stairs up to the house.

2

Jason Cartwright stepped out onto the front porch of the historic house feeling excited about his latest business adventure. He took a deep breath to capture the hot, humid, mountain air as his four-year-old Chesapeake Bay retriever, Zoe, took off after the geese sunning next to the lily pond that sat between the porch and the main road. The property he purchased encompassed nearly fifty acres of mountain land that had been farmed for generations, held impressive banks of hardwoods, and recently had been pulled-back from the dead by its former owner. What was an overgrown drive-by nestled back in the trees for decades now hosted twelve discretely placed, rustic, cabins adorned with higher-end amenities for guests to both enjoy and sometimes use to hide from the world.

Being less than thirty minutes from Asheville and the famous Biltmore Estate, along with having breath-taking views of the Blue Ridge Mountains in every direction, the cabins on the property had great appeal for family trips, couple's escapes, and very private interludes. Jason discovered the farm while renting one of its cabins over Christmas and New Year's seven months earlier while his daughters spent the holidays with their mother. He enjoyed the winter solitude it offered. He spent most of his time in seclusion with many good books, bourbon, and a warm fire. It was during this stay that he met the owner and heard her story.

The vision for the property was impressive and quickly evolved into a lucrative but short-lived enterprise for its founders, Clara and Tom Haigh. The Haigh's moved from Atlanta with a plan to build something unique in the mountains that leveraged their shared expertise in the hospitality business. Tom, however, died unexpectedly a year after they opened from an aggressive pancreatic cancer that not only took his life but also all their life savings. What started as ordinary weakness attributed to the pains of hard, physical work on the property, showed to be far more when Tom could not complete his daily tasks and finally took Clara's advice to see a doctor.

As the bills for the healthcare that insurance did not pay both grew and came due, the Haigh's were forced to remortgage their farm to pay for medical services that kept Tom alive a little longer while killing Clara's livelihood and their dream in the process. The farm was their only child that they created together. It could not die with him.

Jason was immediately impressed with the property when he first drove in through its front gate. Its first impression far exceeded the advertisements that drew him. His plan was that his all-cash purchase that eliminated all debt stress would enable the business to breath and prosper. He also felt that his marketing expertise as a social media expert would build a year-round cabin business for him and his kids to own and enjoy. The product-positioning secret sauce he perfected that enabled him to build a marketing agency that he sold two years ago for $50 million, would be leaned on to deliver again.

The original historic wood clapboard house was the centerpiece of the property and the first thing visitors saw from the road. With a big traditional front porch that encompassed the entire front and some of its sides, the original farmhouse had been brought back from ruin and refurbished to host the office, a few gathering rooms and a small manager's residence currently occupied by the former owner. Meals to include breakfast, brunch, and dinner, were contracted to local chefs and restaurants nearby and delivered by property staff to each cottage in elegant baskets.

Jason hired Clara Haigh to manage the property and to continue to run the business. Clara's service quality during his first stay was impeccable and her impressive resume of hospitality experience gave him the confidence he needed to invest in the property. It also secured his belief that this type and level of lodging would sell to the many different types of tourist who visited the area year-round.

"Care for a cold sweet tea, Jason?" Clara asked as she appeared on the porch from the front door.

Caught deep in thought while comfortably resting in one of the wood rockers that lined the front porch, Jason did not answer. Clara's soft, southern voice, however, did eventually gently pull his attention back from his stare out over the floating pond lilies to her. His fifty-five-year-old body, which was limber and fit from daily ocean swims, had found solid comfort in the stiff support of the shaped wooden chairs that surrounded him as he sat back in a slight recline.

"Jason?" Clara asked again holding the sweating glass of tea in her hand.

Jason's face ignited as he smiled then instinctively stood to her question and to receive the glass of cold tea. Clara Haigh presented as a traditional, casual southern lady with an outer natural beauty that was complemented by a notably authentic southern grace and charm. But what impressed Jason most about Clara was her ability to transition from genteel to a work mode that defined the *whatever it takes* mantra of a good entrepreneur. Clara was not afraid to get dirty.

"Thanks Clara," he said in appreciation of the gesture. "I'm so happy with this. I hope you are too."

Clara looked at Jason with sincere gratitude. She was sad to have sold the property. But she was thankful to him that he came at the time he did and had the interest and resources he had. That combination enabled her to save the business to her vision and to secure her future for as long as she wanted to be there.

"You've taken a load of worry off of me Jason," she answered. "I can only be thankful for that."

Jason smiled feeling good that not only had he made a good investment in something he found interesting and lucrative, but that he also did a good turn for a woman who had suffered too much pain and would have been exploited through a desperate sale of her property. The old Fox Farm was the vision and dream of Clara Haigh and her husband Tom. And at forty-eight years of age, she deserved to live her life there without any extraordinary worry for as long as she wanted.

"So, I guess you'll be heading back to the beach tomorrow to be with your girls?" Clara asked as she settled in the rocker next to him.

There was a sadness in her voice that said she was disappointed that he was leaving. Running the property was never either a bother or challenge for her. It was second nature. But she was growing used to having Jason around. First as a guest through December and the New Year then when he visited again in May to walk the property with his advisors before making his offer.

Like his offer for his beach cottage, some would say he overpaid. The amount he paid to Clara was generous. But the final number was also calculated to produce an investment he could enjoy, revenue from, and pass on to his girls in his estate. Each of them was given a twelve percent stake in the LLC created to own the property and business the moment Jason bought it. It was a defendable ownership number he would joke later still gave him control of the company so he could never be fired.

"I think I'll stay a little bit longer," Jason sighed. "I kind of like it here. No salt, no sun, and no sand to deal with."

"Just bugs," Clara laughed feeling the warmth of a slight blush run across her cheeks.

"Yes," he smirked. "Just bugs."

# # # #

The abrasion on Callie's forearm was more than first expected. Splinters from the wood handrail that embedded under her skin in the fall became visible as she wiped away the initial bleeding with a wet towel. After drying the area for a look, she then applied some expired antiseptic Faith found in Jason's medicine cabinet.

"What's the prognosis doc?" Maya joked as she sat at the kitchen island to watch.

Maya knew the dig on her sister while she was trying to do something nice would annoy her. Faith's serious personality was ripe for embarrassing pokes. This was an ongoing battle the sisters had since they were small children.

"Shut up Maya," Faith answered. "This is a little bit more than what I first expected."

Callie watched as Faith used her thumb to push on the bottom of the splinters that were embedded under the skin. Although painful, Callie knew from experience with her boys that the Faith's efforts were right for now. The hope was that each wood fragment would exit the skin through the same hole they entered. Once exposed, Faith used tweezers she sterilized in Jason's Tito's Vodka. It was an added step to ensure the right level disinfecting properties in case the antiseptic failed.

"Did you sterilize the field?" Maya laughed.

"Shut… up… Maya," Faith answered in a stern, slow, cadence without taking her eyes off her surgical field.

Callie trusted that Faith's efforts would be successful. But she could not bear to watch the process. With Maya sitting comfortably only a few feet away, Callie's only option was to either look up and out into the small living room or through the sliding glass doors that showed the ocean view. As she scanned the room, Callie found comfort in seeing some of the art that she and Jason had purchased together almost thirty years ago. The photo Faith mentioned, that was in reach on the kitchen counter, did not offer the comfort she hoped it would. Although it was distracting, as expected, it was not a good picture of her. A final tug on her skin followed by a triumphant *"woooolah"* by Faith announced that the last splinter had been removed.

"Let that air dry for a second," Faith commanded. "I'll be right back."

Callie waved her arm back and forth to dry the antiseptic Faith applied before she disappeared back into the hallway that led to the three bedrooms. Faith quickly returned to the operating site with several sealed packets of gauze and some white athletic tape. The injury field was larger than a Band-Aid could cover comfortably.

"These extra gauze pads are for later," Faith explained. "You should probably swap them out in an hour or so because they'll stick to any drying blood."

Callie smiled at the instructions she was receiving from the twenty-one-year-old, hopeful, medical student. Faith's serious demeanor showed a dedication that was going to work well in her future craft. Faith also had the same maturity Callie saw in Maya during her visit in October.

"Where'd you learn to do this?" Callie asked.

Faith maintained a serious look as her eyes moved from the wound she was dressing to Callie's.

"I'm a lifeguard at home," she answered confidently. "We're all lifeguards. So, we all know first aid. But we also played competitive soccer where muddy, turf-burned, raspberries, like this, but mostly on my butt, were more the norm than not."

"You're being treated by the queen of the slide tackle," Maya interjected.

"Well, then I'm in good hands."

Callie's boys played competitive lacrosse through high school.

Her daughter Lizzie played soccer briefly at the local club level. She was familiar with the injuries and terms used for abrasions and cuts.

Faith returned her focus to disposing of the medical waste she created. A quick wash off her hand over the kitchen's electric garbage can opened its lid. It was a novelty that Faith made fun of when she first used it. But now the sterile distance it offered her hands was appreciated.

Callie took a moment to observe the two girls as they continued with their activities. Maya's face was buried in her phone screen while two-thumbing a message or post to someone. Faith walked the disinfectant back to the bathroom where it belonged along with a few of the extra gauze packets that were not needed. She left the tape behind to secure the second round of gauze.

As the activity settled in the room, the glass door facing the beach filled with motion and conversation as it slid open. Leading the pack of young, fit, adult bodies was a shorter in stature, twenty-five-year-old girl in a skimpy bikini and some sunburn. Her comfort, look, and shoulder length chestnut hair ponytailed under a baseball cap told Callie that she was one of the last two Cartwright daughters she had to meet.

"Oh, hello," Rachel declared as she was surprised by Callie's presence in the room. "I'm Rachel."

Rachel's shock to see someone her mom's age was obvious as she extended her hand out to Callie. Her eyes then began to float to the picture that sat on the counter next to Callie then back to Callie. As Rachel began to put together who the strange woman in the house was, Callie spoke.

"Hi Rachel. I'm Callie"

Rachel was mesmerized by the marvel of actually meeting the mystery woman in the photo.

"I'm her," Callie added as she pointed to the picture.

Maya and Faith smiled at each other as Rachel's expression remained frozen as she processed through what she had just learned. This was her dad's love interest from last fall who he would not talk about.

The three boys who entered with Rachel all stood in silence as they watched and waited for something to happen. Anticipating that Rachel would make introductions at some point, Callie gave each a glance and a smile to acknowledge their presence.

"Rachel!" Maya interjected. "Introduce the guys."

The names of the three young men flew past Callie as she became overwhelmed by the presence of Jason's three vastly different daughters and their friends. Two of the boys were wearing Virginia Tech shirts. Both had buzz-cut hair that likely meant they were enrolled as cadets. They were most likely Faith's friends. The third boy was wearing a *Go Cocks!* t-shirt with the University of South Carolina inscribed underneath it. Callie knew that Rachel, despite now living in Austin, Texas, graduated from South Carolina a few years ago. The boy wearing the Gamecock swag looked older than the others and was likely a friend of hers.

As everyone disbursed to both the bathroom and available chairs, Rachel moved to settle into the kitchen. She pulled a large pitcher from under the counter and filled it halfway with ice from the icemaker Jason had installed under the island. Callie watched wondering as Rachel's approach to what she was doing was very deliberate and systematic. When she grabbed the bottle of Jose Cuervo tequila, Callie began to get a sense of where everything was heading.

Rachel emptied the fifth of tequila into the pitcher of ice. She then topped it off with the Margarita mix that Maya had purchased earlier on her store run. The mix looked to be fifty-fifty and filled the pitcher. Rachel completed her effort with a stir of the concoction with a wooden spoon and the presentation of a stack of red Solo cups.

"I don't think we're going to have enough," she observed as she looked straight at Callie with a smug expression.

"I won't be drinking," Callie answered while waving her hand to decline.

As she did, Faith's bandaging of Callie's arm came into view. Rachel's notice of the clean, very white gauze told her that the dressing was fresh.

"That looks like it hurts," Rachel responded while lifting the first cup into action. "You get the first one."

Rachel poured margarita as a few ice cubes splashed with it into a cup. Callie's first inclination was to decline the drink. She had a two-hour drive back to Williamsburg ahead of her and drinking before leaving would make a bad first impression. But this was Rachel's first welcoming gesture to her that she did not want to refuse. Callie accepted the cup with a smile and took a taste. The heavy load of Tequila hit her taste buds forcing her to work hard to maintain a normal facial expression.

"Good, isn't it?" Rachel asked as she started to build her assembly line of cups to pour drinks for everyone.

By the time Callie was able to speak again, Rachel's full attention was focused back on her process of delivering Margaritas to everyone. She sat back to watch the rest of the group all settled into their seats, with phones illuminated, while waiting for their happy-hour refreshment to arrive. The light in the cottage was better for reading screens than the beach. As Callie became accustomed to the strength of Rachel's first pour, she quickly realized her drink was nearing empty before everyone else had been served theirs.

# # # #

Clara had disappeared back into the house as Jason returned

from his car with his phone. He had a bad habit of leaving it in the holder his kids had given him so he could enjoy his Spotify, audio books, and podcasts as he drove. As a result of this forgetfulness, it was not uncommon for either a text or call to their dad to not be answered for hours because of the phone having been left in his car. The girls eventually accepted the fact that delayed replies were not him ignoring them. He was just forgetting to grab his phone after a drive. Out of sight meant out of mind. Jason called it the cellular transitive property of equality. It was a geometry joke that only he seemed to get.

Jason scrolled through his emails as he walked up the steps then instinctively sat back down in the rocker he had left moments ago. He noticed Clara was gone as he returned thinking she had been called into the house to hopefully answer a call seeking to make a reservation. He knew he could hear phone conversations at the front desk from where he was seated on the front porch. The sound of clanking dishes indicated she was in the kitchen.

The business up until now had been good and trending stronger. His marketing efforts that started back in late spring were beginning to pay dividends. As part of the effort, he continued all the traditional paths of the various lodging websites along with Airbnb which he found particularly useful. His property was a destination rather than just a place to lay heads while traveling from point A to point B. It was miles from the nearest highway which made the surroundings both tranquil and not easy to simply *run into.*

The biggest opportunity to date was a contact made by a location scout for a romantic comedy movie being shot that required a mountain setting similar to the property. The potential from a mass audience seeing the farm and its cabins was easy to recognize. The uncertainty of the timing and the length of time his cabins would be occupied for the shoot, and everything else that came along with it, was bothering him. For a movie to be shot on his property, he would have to shut everything down and open space on lawns for trailers and other trappings. Despite being in the early stages of the inquiry, Jason's protective nature was beginning to influence his adventurous side.

"Here we go," Clara announced as she backed slowly through the screen door.

In her hands, she was carrying a tray of neatly cut cheeses and crackers. She turned to walk slowly toward Jason to set it all on the small table that rested next to his rocker. Without pause, Jason scooped up the small table to put it out in front of their chairs for easy access by both of them.

As Clara nestled into her own rocker next to his, Jason put his phone on the rocker's flat wooden arm as he gave Clara a smile of appreciation. The variety of cheeses were sophisticated and inviting from tastes of soft gouda to a hard, white cheddar. The wafers were thin and crisp with a complementing dryness to the cheese.

"You're spoiling me," Jason said. "I'm kinda scared to see my final bill for my stay."

Clara gave him a glance with a smirk as she reached to prepare her own snack.

"It's on the house," she declared.

Clara knew, if she was being honest with herself, that Jason was remarkably similar in nature and appearance to her husband Tom. He had the same down-to-earth, creative, and hands-on approach to just about everything. He also had an innate smartness she found attractive. His ability to calm even the most frustrating situations impressed her on several occasions during the sale and working with some of the local contractors and vendors to the property.

"But, don't think I won't make you work for it," Clara added hesitantly eager to see his reaction.

Jason was her guest and friend before he became her boss. The chain-of-command on the property was set and obvious. She could not, however, resist the opportunity to test his interests beyond just owning Fox Farms.

The response she received to her trial balloon was neither encouraging nor disappointing. He gave a brief smile to the insinuation as he chewed on his wafer and cheese. He was clearly enjoying the treat he was tasting and did not seem to mind the company he was keeping. Something was obviously stirring in Jason's mind as he worked to swallow his appetizer.

"We're going to be a good team," he said.

Clara could not hold eye contact with him as a smile followed his comment. There was something starting to gel that she was not quite sure if she either wanted or thought was a good idea. It was the first time since meeting her husband that she saw opportunity in another man. Her better judgment wondered if it was only because Jason was her white knight at the darkest time in her life; or, if it was because he was so much like Tom. She wanted to be sure before hoping for anything. Her future was with him in some capacity. Whether it was as employer, friend and/or lover remained to be seen.

3

Callie let time slip by as she became captivated with Jason's girls and their friends. She saw in them her own two sons and daughter bantering about during their family vacations spent in Nantucket up until this year when she was not invited to go. The differences in the three girls was obvious. It made her laugh and think about the individuality she saw in each of her own kids despite having the same mom and dad gene mix. The group made a joint decision to move outside as the sun continued to soften during its drift toward the western horizon. The resulting soft, warm orange glow was far more tolerable than its midday blistering heat.

Despite Rachel's declaration that the first pitcher of margarita's was not going to be enough, a second fifth of Jose Cuervo appeared from under the counter just as the last drop poured from the first pitcher. Callie laughed with the group to the SURPRISE discovery that she knew Rachel had planned long before coming in for happy hour. The same fifty-fifty mix was portioned in the second pitcher. Callie was beginning to feel the numbing effects of the first round when Rachel refilled her glass without asking.

"I don't think I should drink this. I've got a two-hour drive back to Williamsburg."

"Do you have anywhere you have to be tomorrow?" Rachel asked in her usual direct fashion as if knowing Callie's visit was not to just to pop in on her dad.

Her directness surprised Callie. She tried to contemplate an answer that would get her on her way when she noticed that all the conversation in the room had stopped; and, that everyone was looking at her waiting on an answer. The amused looks on their faces presented an invitation to stay quelling her initial anxious feeling to the question.

"No. I really don't," Callie laughed.

"Then, drink up!" Rachel exclaimed.

"And know that you won't be in any condition to drive after this social!" the three daughters shouted together.

The saying was familiar to Callie. It mocked Jason's friend Rebecca who Callie had met in October. Rebecca had made the same declaration at Callie's first Abbie's happy hour.

Rebecca's ancestry dated back to the founding and development of the island. Although in her mid-forties, she took on the self-appointed role of mother-hen. Rebecca did her thing well to carefully help Callie and Jason manage the time and effects of their unplanned weekend last October.

Callie laughed remembering Rebecca's first *social* warning of the Abbie Happy Hour after-effects. She was feeling comfortable with Jason's family and back on the bench where so much was confessed and uncovered ten months earlier. For the first time, in a long time, Callie was calm and feeling good that things in her life were going to be fine.

Callie would never admit it. But her experience with Jason's daughters created a strange sensation similar to a schoolgirl being accepted into the *cool clique*. It was a subtle elation that overrode the sadness she was feeling that she was not hanging out with her own kids in a similar beach setting. But with her oldest teaching English in Spain, and the other two in Nantucket with their father, their D.C. McMansion, that was now for sale, was empty of life. She had nowhere to be.

Over the past several months, the empty house became more familiar and less of bother. Chase moved out in February, right before Valentine's Day. It was on that day, she finally decided to move forward with the divorce. Although having family money and her expected divorce settlement, she knew it was not in her best interest to keep the house. That place had to be put behind her too. Her sadness to sell was not rooted in missing the wonderful home that painfully reminded her of him. It was missing the home where her children grew up compounded by the stress of where to land next. Her daughter, Lizzie's, attachment to her friends, along with Jason's experience with his kids after he moved away after his divorce, indicated that leaving the D.C. area would be even more isolating and painful than staying in the home.

"Rachel?" called a familiar voice from down below on the sand.

Its soft southern hue grabbed Callie's ear as she instinctively stood to look down at the unexpected visitor.

"Well, hello, old friend," Rebecca called out as she immediately started up the stairs.

The three girls, surprised by Rebecca's response, looked at each other then back at the impending reunion between the *two old friends*. There was no hesitation in Rebecca to climb the stairs to give Callie a warm, welcoming hug. Being a few inches taller and surrounded by a light beach cover, Rebecca's embrace consumed Callie's smaller frame. The two were visibly happy to see each other which made the three girls even more curious to the depth of their friendship and what exactly happened last fall.

"I'm excited to see you here," Rebecca said as she pulled back to look. "I'd ask you how things are but…. I'm sure *we can talk about that later*…. YOU'RE HERE! So, all is good…"

Rebecca's elated face scanned the blank expressions looking back her from the benches.

"And I see you've started happy hour without me," she smiled.

"Care for a libation?" Maya posed sarcastically.

"Thought you'd never offer," she answered as Rachel handed her a solo cup already filled in anticipation of her answer.

The heightened attention by the group on the deck became uncomfortable as Callie and Rebecca each took a drink. Rebecca's eyes, nod, and a toast of her cup to Rachel expressed her appreciation for the quality of the drink Rachel had crafted.

"Muy Bueno," she added following her first swallow.

Sensing a need to separate Callie from Jason's girls, Rebecca invited her for a beach walk to *catch up* as well as to save her from the inquisition that was either happening or about to happen. The two friends quickly exited down the stairs out on to the sand with their topped-off margaritas. Molly decided to stay with the girls and their friends for any potential food that may appear.

# # # #

The foamy, salt water that washed across her feet was notably warmer than what she remembered from October. The sun that baked the shoreline earlier had lost its intense heat as its rich warm orange glow illuminated the homes. Although their meeting on the deck in front of Jason's girls was full of excitement and desire to talk, the start of their next conversation lagged as each waited for the other to speak first.

As she watched each foot sink into the foam and sand, Callie remembered her first sighting of Rebecca in October when she thought Rebecca was a potential love interest for Jason. She was walking with a pack of middle-aged women all clad in bright beach covers. Rebecca's tall and lean body immediately stood out and stirred some jealousy in Callie when she strayed over to talk to him. And despite believing she was happily married at the time, Callie smiled when she recalled thinking back then that *of course she's the pretty, tall, lean one and not one of the rounder models.*

"So," Rebecca exhaled. "Where to start."

Callie found humor and comfort in the opening as she was pondering the same thought. Rebecca's question was intentionally open-ended. As a physician, she expected Callie had news and needed to exhaust her anxiety through talking with a trusted friend. And despite the fact that she and Rebecca only knew each other for a brief moment back in October, Rebecca was confident that both the separation she had from Callie's life, along with the bond they had from formed in the fall, made her someone Callie could confide in with confidence that it would go no further.

"I don't know what to say," Callie answered slowly. "It certainly feels right to be here."

The diversion from the question confirmed Rebecca's thinking that she was right to extend Callie an ear. Healing happens in many ways. Regardless of who harmed whom in the process of Callie's marriage, neither she nor Chase were going to exit without pain and a need for support from the outside. Callie may have come looking for Jason as her sounding board. But Rebecca knew that she was better suited as a woman, a physician, and as a relatively disinterested outsider to be Callie's first touch back into his life.

"You don't have to tell me anything," Rebecca replied to reduce any pressure on her. "We've had a busy summer here. Unfortunately, another cottage sold over the winter that's going to be replaced with another atrocious monstrosity that just isn't this place. At least what it once was."

Rebecca's sadness on the loss of a cottage she did not own paled in comparison to Callie's marital implosion. Although the word divorce was never stated, Callie's presence at Jason's said it for her. Callie did empathize with the cottage loss knowing its importance to Rebecca, the Abbies, and to Jason. But to her, it was just a smaller version of something that could be bigger. Her history of renting houses for her family in Nantucket always skewed to the larger homes with the most modern amenities and nicer accommodations.

"He cheated on me," Callie said softly. "My husband, fucking, cheated on me. And it's been going on for years... Once he finally confessed to it, it was like he was gleeful to keep hurting me with it."

Rebecca stopped as she heard the declaration. Her disapproval of Callie's visit in the fall was kept to herself. She trusted that Jason acted as she expected him to which would have kept that visit proper. Her read of Callie, given their very brief time together, was the same.

"I'm so sorry to hear that," Rebecca replied softly. "You don't have to explain anything to me."

"It's ok. It's all out there now," Callie replied. "My kids even know. As part of the marriage counseling, he had to admit it to them then apologize to all of us. I was so embarrassed. The worst part was actually telling my mother."

Rebecca began to see that her sensing of Callie's need to talk was right. Through the rest of their walk, Callie painted the entire picture of infidelity during Chase's travels that he blamed partially on campaign loneliness and on Callie's coldness when he was home. Coldness that was due mostly to child-induced exhaustion.

Chase also used the excitement of each campaign and the new relationships they offered as sometimes too much to refuse, particularly when it came time to celebrate wins. The added judgement loss when drinking started some of his affairs that lasted from one-night stands to months until his job was done. His most recent affair with a thirty-five-year-old Senate staffer from Florida had firmer footing and lasted over a year. Chase broke that off after catching Callie with Jason in October.

Despite his wandering eye and infidelities, Chase's reluctance to leave Callie for the woman he spent a year hiding was rooted in the same concrete commitments Callie said she made to him, their family, and to God on the day they married. Callie did not mention if she had made any confessions for her weekend with Jason last fall. Rebecca knew Chase already knew. So, she did not ask.

As they returned to Jason's cottage, both looked to see the empty bench area above the dune lit by the deeper orange tone of the sun on the bayside horizon. Callie smiled in appreciation to Rebecca as both realized it was time to separate. Rebecca was already late to get back to her family and to their dinner. Callie knew she was three strong drinks in on her one-hundred-and-twenty-pound body. A consideration she did not want to have with a two hour drive back to her mom's in Williamsburg. Although she did not feel drunk, she did know she was compromised to drive.

"Where are you staying?" Rebecca asked.

"I'm heading back to Williamsburg."

"I wouldn't advise that."

Callie smiled to the advice while touching Rebecca's arm. She felt able to drive and needed to pull away from the beach and people she desperately wanted to both meet and see only if Jason had been there.

"I'm sure the girls would let you crash in Jason's bedroom," Rebecca offered for him. "I'd offer but we have kids on couches as it is.... One of the bonuses of small cottage living."

Callie understood the comment and replied with only a frustrated smirk. There was a certain irony to the fact that Jason's bed would be empty on the day she returned looking for him. Although she did have a bag in her car packed for a longer stay in either Williamsburg with her mom or at the beach in one of Jason's guest rooms, she wasn't sure what the best decision was for the night since he wasn't there to extend an invitation.

"I'm sure they would," Callie finally confessed. "I'm also sure it would also lead to some awkward conversations."

Rebecca smiled while nodding in agreement. None of Jason's daughters were shy about either talking to anyone or seeking information they wanted to know. Jason had an innate ability to uncover details quietly without being intrusive. It was a quality Rebecca appreciated because, as a physician, she sometimes had to deploy the same tactics with reluctant patients. It was also how she uncovered most of Jason's history when they first met. Everything except his failed engagement twenty-eight years ago to Callie. A detail he left out of his life story despite his inclusion of Callie's parental decay philosophy through a family's progression of children.

The youngest always gets away with murder because their older siblings collectively wear down mom and dad to nothing.

"Just be careful… and safe," Rebecca added. "We have more drinks to drink, and laughs to laugh, in our future here in God's country."

Callie radiated to the warmth of Rebecca's goodbye. Rebecca's declaration that Callie should not be driving back to Williamsburg added its intended weight. As she walked up the stairs and the house came into view, Callie noted that the boys were nowhere to be seen; and, that Rachel and Faith were busy preparing food in the kitchen. Callie had fifty steps to decide what she was going to do. To drive back to Williamsburg was ill-advised, dangerous, and would send the wrong message to Jason's kids. Staying at the house, in his bed, seemed to send a similar message she did not want to deal with either now or throughout the evening to come.

# # # #

The sounds of summer filled the air as Jason settled into his cabin. The *Flying Dutchman* was not reserved for the week and was his favorite of the farm's twelve retreats. It sat high above the hillside with a deck and view that looked out into and over the dense trees. Despite the high heat and humidity of summer, Jason kept his sliding door open with the accompanying screen door shut to keep the bugs out.

Alone for the first time, Jason nestled into an old Shaker-style reading chair that sat next to the glass wall next to the deck. The orange hue that lit the sky filtered peacefully from behind and through the forest that surrounded him. The day had been easy with errands and strategy conversations with Clara. He left her back at the main house happier with his choice to both buy the property and to hire her as its general manager. Done for the day, Jason took a sip of Roughrider bourbon he had brought from his own stash and poured into one of the cabin's cut crystal glasses. He then took a moment to start thinking about dinner.

Undecided on what to do, Jason took a final swig of Roughrider then closed his eyes as its heat worked through his gumline. The room temperature was soothing as the sounds of everything natural around him lulled him into subconscious thought where his mind could go blank. As he finally reached a complete state of relaxation, a knock sounded on his door launching Zoe from rest beside him and into full bark mode. Still in a fog, he stood to go greet the visitor at the door.

Just outside each cabin door was a wooden cabinet lined with a sealed, stainless-steel container. The cabinets were designed by Clara after their initial guests complained about animals enjoying dinners before their guests had a chance to find them. Her husband Tom suggested the stainless liners for sanitary reasons and their thermal features. He then built Clara attractive wood boxes around them that matched the cottages. A flippable marker was on the door to indicate when a meal was inside.

When Jason opened the door, no one was there to greet him. He stepped out onto the small landing to look around catching a sight of Clara driving the camp's John Deere Gator off into the trees. Quickly glancing at the cabinet, he saw dinner had been delivered.

"CLARA!" he shouted followed by a piercing whistle he developed while coaching girls' soccer.

As the cart disappeared, Jason looked to see if something had been delivered or, worse, a meal for some other guest was mistakenly left at the *Flying Dutchman*. When he opened the cabinet, he found two covered dishes complimented with a bottle of Cabernet. Confused, he immediately reached for his phone to get Clara back so that the right guest would get their meal.

Jason let the phone ring a number of times before giving up. As he started a text regarding the dinners, he heard the rumble of the Gator coming back over the road then saw Clara at the wheel. Despite her shoulder length hair blowing back in the wind, he noticed she looked different as she came to a stop at his cottage.

"I think you delivered meals to me that were supposed to go to someone else," Jason stated as Clara slowly dismounted from the cart.

Her walk was unusually hesitant questioning whether she should fess up to a mistake that did not happen or tell the truth.

"I'm sorry," she said. "I wasn't thinking."

Clara's disposition was shyer than usual which made Jason uncomfortable.

"I just don't want this to go to waste. Or, for anyone to be mad about a late, cold dinner"

"I'm sorry Jason. It was just a bad idea."

Clara's comment confirmed Jason's impression of what was unfolding. And, to him, at this point in time, and given their business relationship, it was a *bad idea*.

"What's a bad idea?' Jason asked wondering if asking was a *good idea*.

Embarassed by her action, Clara smiled shyly before speaking.

"I'd thought we'd have dinner together," she finally confessed. "We've been working on business so much that I thought a simple, casual dinner would be fun and good for our relationship."

Clara's voice fell off as she thought about the use of the word *relationship*. Deep down, she meant it as he heard it. But she was hopeful that he heard it more as a friendly gesture.

"I thought you were kind of getting tired of me sticking my nose in your business all day," Jason answered. "We could've gone out to a nice lakeside dinner instead... My treat."

The mountain village of Lake Lure was less than fifteen minutes from the cottages. That distance increased the appeal for the Fox Farm cottages as a destination because Lake Lure, Asheville and The Biltmore were all close, but still far enough away from the summer crowds.

Clara saw a quick mental vision of her at a table with Jason that overlooked the lake at sunset. A twinge of disappointment pitted in her stomach as she thought to save the effort for their dinner at his cottage.

"Can I have a rain-check on that?" she asked.

Jason smiled happy to see confidence reappear in her face.

"Absolutely," he answered. "Claim it any time I'm here. Now, let's see what's for dinner."

As Clara took her first steps toward him, Jason unlatched the cabinet to open the door to the waiting dinner and wine. He handed the bottle to her as she stood near him then grabbed the tray to move their dinner inside. As he watched her enter through the door, Clara presented in a dramatically different fashion than she had before. Up until this point, she was his employee and a widow to be respected. But the social gesture to have dinner just to spend time together changed his impression of her. She was showing an attractive grace and charm he had not fully appreciated until now.

"Oh," Clara said in an urgent tone that brought Jason back to normal thought. "Did you text your girls that you were staying? You said you didn't want to forget that."

Jason chuckled as he took a moment to realign his thoughts. He then smiled in embarrassment to what he had just been thinking.

"No, I haven't," he admitted. "I'll do that now before I forget again."

4

Their phones all chimed at different times with different *dad tones* that lasted several seconds. The fact that they either did not or could not ring at the same time had irritated Rachel since they all got cell phones as kids. Had hers always been first to ring, it would not have been a problem. But as the oldest, and the first to get a phone, she always felt hers should chime first when a group text arrived rather than seconds after most of the others received theirs.

"Dad's staying a few more days!" Faith announced as Callie knocked on the sliding glass door.

"Well, that's not good news," Rachel answered. "I hope he left money or a credit card. I'm not paying to feed you guys."

"Not a problem, I'll just use mine with his name on it," Faith answered as she waved Callie in and continued her dinner preparations.

"Callie…. Can I call you that?" Faith inquired. "I don't know your last name."

Callie smiled at the comment and the realization of how little Jason's girls knew about her.

"Callie's fine," she answered knowing that would bug Jason. "I just came in to say goodbye."

Maya walked in from the hallway to sit on an island stool as Rachel and Faith stopped their work at the comment.

"Why don't you stay for dinner?" Rachel offered. "We have enough."

"I should go," Callie answered. "Thank you though. That's very nice."

"Oh, come on. You won't get home until later anyway and will have to eat on your way back," Maya added knowing Callie's desire to get away from them. "What's a few hours. You're welcome to stay if you'd like. My dad would insist on that."

Callie smiled as she thought through the offer. As she looked at each of their faces, she noted a hope that she would at least stay for dinner. And before she could reply, Rachel had a glass of chardonnay poured and offered as an added incentive. At this point, Callie felt cornered and committed. Resisting was only going to add to more awkwardness to when they would meet again.

"I'd love to," Callie finally declared.

She accepted the glass of wine graciously with a nervous laugh. She knew adding the wine to her three solo cups of Margarita was going to be problematic for a drive back to Williamsburg. Instinctively, she took a drink to offset the mounting anxiety that thought produced. Deep down, she knew she would be sleeping in Jason's bed tonight.

# # # #

The back deck on the Flying Dutchman hovered twenty-two feet above the sloping hillside. A square table that could seat four was nestled into a corner. The rest of the surface hosted a small love seat and chair in the middle and a two-person hot tub in the far corner. The positioning of the hot tub was intentional to eliminate all lines of sight for privacy.

As Clara removed dinner from the basket, Jason rooted through the small kitchen for utensils, wine glasses, and a corkscrew. Their timing back to the table was perfect as Jason created both place-settings and uncorked the bottle of Cabernet to air. Clara had already lit the citronella candles strategically placed on each rail post for their soft light and to help keep any flying nuisances at bay.

"I'm glad you thought of this," Jason said. "We should do this more often. And, I should've thought of it first. *I... apologize.*"

Jason's failed attempt at a southern accent made Clara smile. It was a quirkiness she appreciated and eerily put as another similarity to her husband Tom. A sadness then began to weigh on her as Jason helped her be seated then sat in the chair across from hers.

Clara was reluctant to be the first one to speak. But when the silence between them became too much, she said the first thing that came to mind.

"I think for marketing that we should..."

"Stop," Jason smiled while putting his hand on hers. "This is social. Tell me about your childhood."

The sincerity in Jason's request was real; although, it was also common to most conversations he would start with strangers. *Tell me something about yourself* was a great way to put people at ease. He felt that aside from the fact that all people really like their own ideas, the easiest way to get someone comfortable and relaxed was to get them to talk about something comfortable and relaxed. Most of the time, the tactic worked. But there were a few times it did not. His read on Clara was that her warm-and-fuzzy topic was her childhood.

Clara's story was not much different than what he observed with his four girls as they grew from babies to girls to young women. The inquisitiveness, the successes, and the failures, although in different things and at different times, seemed remarkably similar on a high level. Clara shared the first time she drank alcohol at a high school party. Without a ride home, she had to call her dad to be picked up. As she stumbled out the front door of the house without any courageous friends to help her, her dad sat in the car amused as she fought the inclination to fall with short steps and frequent pauses to regain her balance. As she climbed in the front seat, her father turned serious with two questions. "Did you have a good time?" And, "do you have something to tell me?"

Clara answered *yes* to one of her dad's questions and *no* to the other. On the way home, the car had to stop so she could get sick. The next morning her dad gave her the only "pass" he said he was going to give because she called him. Jason's immediate thought was to the same thing happening with several of his own daughters. One chose not to call and did not get the usual pass for pushing the rules of the house. Jason's telling of his like experiences with his girls was comforting to Clara. Any man that survived raising four daughters certainly had the *patience of Job* and stories to tell. It was becoming clear to her why he was so successful along with why she was finding him more and more attractive as a man.

The stories of life from Jason's childhood, Clara's, and his kids built upon each other until the last glass of wine was split marking the coming end to the dinner and their evening. They had spent two hours talking that passed like minutes. Their thoughts and laughs flowed together seamlessly. There were no surprises unearthed by either of them as their familiarity with the other grew.

"Thanks so much for dinner," Jason finally said appreciative of Clara's effort to get to know him.

Clara gave an acknowledging smile as she thought she should be thanking him. As the owner, he paid for it. But she held back the thought in case that qualification would kill the mood.

"This was fun," she answered while standing to clear plates back into the basket. Her hope was that he would invite her to stay around a little longer.

"We'll have to do this again. There's no point in either of us eating alone when I'm here."

The thought that he thought of the dinner like that took the happiness of the evening out of her. Her eyes began to well with tears as she turned to face away from him. And although she was able to hold off the drop of even one tear, she took a moment to regain her composure before replying.

"Absolutely," she answered while lifting the full basket.

Jason noted the change in her demeanor and asked if he had said something wrong.

"No," she answered. "I do need to get these plates back and to pick up the others so they can be clean for tomorrow."

Jason knew that plate pick-up was in the morning and that Clara was trying to make a quick exit. He knew digging deeper would unroot things he did not, rather could not, have come between them. Fox Farm was a business to run. He needed Clara to run it; or, his great investment could hit a wall.

"Ok," he said quietly. "Let me carry this out to the Gator so you can get on your way."

As they exited the cottage and Jason placed the basket into the bed of the Gator, Clara's chatty self was dead quiet.

"Let me drive you back," he said to cut the silence. "I'll circle back in the morning and do pick-up with you."

Jason regretted the offer the moment he said it. To offer pick-up assistance let Clara know that he knew she was running away from him. Clara stood for a moment to contemplate her next statement. But instead of words she just leaned in and kissed him lightly on the cheek.

"I'm good," she said with a head-tilt and forced smile. "Thanks for dinner.... boss."

A smile erupted on her face as she abruptly backed away and jumped into the Gator. Jason wore a befuddled look as he waved appreciating the simultaneous warmth and jab. In his mind and through a subtle lean, he expected to kiss her. This fun quality was something he saw and appreciated in Clara when they first met. It was also a quality he loved about Callie when she squared-off against an awkward situation.

# # # #

Rachel and Faith's dinner concoction was shrimp scampi. The girl's ability to prepare a tasty main course of seafood along with a complimenting salad impressed Callie. Meals from her twenties were simpler and not as good. After almost thirty years, Jason continued to tease her about her chicken and broccoli fail from when they were dating.

As plates were being gathered, Callie noticed that the four of them had consumed two bottles of Jason's Chardonnay. She did not keep a count on her number of glasses. But she was feeling light-headed from the effects of the wine and the earlier margaritas. She could not tell if any of the three college-age girls felt the same way despite having consumed the same amount of alcohol, if not more.

Callie instinctively stood to go wash dishes. In her house, whether on vacation or at home, her kids would scatter, and Chase would find something important to address on his phone like sexting his homewrecking whores. But as she stood thinking about that with plates in her hand, she was stopped by Faith who immediately took them from her.

"You're our guest, please sit down, and enjoy yourself."

Surprised by the unexpected offer, Callie released her grasp of the plates and utensils into Faith's hands. Sitting back down to the empty table felt awkward. So, she moved to sit on a stool at the kitchen island so everyone could keep talking.

"If you don't mind," Callie said. "Can I still take you up on your offer to stay?"

Rachel stopped rinsing plates to look at Faith. Faith's serious expression shifted to a stunted smile as both were thinking the same thing. This was their opportunity to loosen Callie up a little bit more to get background on who she was and why their dad was so interested in her.

"Our dad would insist that you'd stay. He'd likely even be mad if we let you drive away."

Rachel intentionally left out the *since you've been drinking* comment she was thinking. The door of opportunity to learn a lot about her was opening; and she wanted Callie to feel welcome.

"Great, thank you," Callie answered. "Since he's coming back tomorrow, I'll just wait to see him then."

Maya was listening from the living room as Callie spoke. Faith and Rachel could see her behind Callie bouncing up and down in a silent laughter. One of them had to tell Callie that their dad just delayed his return by a few days. It took a few moments before Faith finally broke the silence and shared that news with her. Callie's excitement to have committed to stay vanished.

The hours that followed up until final bedtime were not as tenuous as Callie had feared. The girls were inquisitive on her history with their dad, her life and family in Washington, and her thoughts on their dad thirty years after they last spoke. She was careful not to drill into either the reasons their engagement failed or to talk about anything marital for either Jason or herself. As Chase would advise his political clients, she kept her answers *very high level and conceptual* with just enough to touch on the question without giving any real answer. The girls went to bed comfortable that they had the information they wanted until they mentally retraced back through it all wondering if they got anything at all.

Before going to bed, Callie took a moment alone with Maya to catch-up on the spring and summer. She talked about the family trip she had taken with her family to the Biltmore a few years back and how much she loved that area. Callie added in the fact that she could see why Jason would be attracted to that area trying to throw a few seeds to see if she could uncover where he was without asking. Maya's love of creating sport out of awkward conversations came to an end when Callie could not figure her way past her roadblocks to her dad.

"Do you just want to ask me where he is?" Maya asked with a forgiving smile.

The offer stunned Callie. She believed she was in control of the conversation leading Maya to disclose the whereabouts of her dad when the question came.

"How long did you know I was rooting around for that?" she asked.

Maya did not hesitate to show her amusement with Callie's surprise and frustration. It was clear that Callie knew she was stuck to stay at the house until morning. The fact that they could run the conversation deep into the evening and almost close it out without telling his location was too much to expect. One of sisters was going to break. Like Jason, none of them wanted Callie to miss what she came to find. But, also like Jason, there was devilish sport in making Callie work for the information rather than just giving it to her.

"I wasn't going to tell you until I saw that your rings were gone with no tan lines," Maya said with a quick glance to Callie's left hand.

"Yes," Callie replied with noted relief for the privacy. "That's now over. And it *sucked* just like you said it would last fall and winter."

"You certainly took your time," Maya answered, surprising Callie with the directness. "My dad will appreciate that."

Maya's follow-up comment gave Callie great comfort. It also brought back her appreciation for Maya's advanced maturity at such a young age.

"My dad's at a place called Fox Farm. He stayed there last winter. He's been really secretive about going up there. I know he's been back several times since Christmas when he stayed there for about a month."

Callie knew she could Google the farm when she had opportunity. That Jason spent some of the winter in the mountains surprised her when he said he was likely heading to Florida. Callie accepted Maya's explanation without an expression of either surprise or disappointment.

"That's so *your dad*" she then replied glibly to confirm her understanding of his nature.

As the girls all retreated to bed, Callie and Molly stayed up a little bit longer to walk out to the bench where she and Jason rediscovered each other in October. The air was still hot and humid. It was comforting along with the cadence of the waves crashing on the shoreline. Molly scratched at the closed gate to the sand which Callie instinctively opened for her to visit before going to bed.

As she rested on the familiar bench confident Molly would stay close and return, Callie Googled *Fox Farm near Asheville* to find its website and address. The first picture of vast mountain scenery appeared followed by rotating images of the cottages, the Biltmore Estate, Asheville, and Lake Lure. As Callie thumbed through the cabin offerings, she thought it would have been the type of place she and Chase would have visited had they made it to empty-nest travel. She then read the story about Clara and Tom Haigh's vision to resurrect the historic property into higher-end cabin offering. That Jason would stay there made sense. Callie then took note of Clara's natural beauty as she stood in very casual, but fitting, country attire. Maya did not speculate on why Jason was at Fox Farm in between Ashville and Lake Lure. But it was a question she thought of as she continued to look at Clara Haigh.

5

Callie's plan was to wake early before the house and to sneak out leaving a note of thanks to the girls. As the sun rose, the stripe of light that was created by a gap in the blinds last fall that woke her both mornings, reappeared earlier than expected and had the same effect. The house seemed still asleep as she quietly visited the bathroom, packed her bag, and headed down the hallway. As she entered the living room looking for a pen and paper, she was surprised to not be the only one up.

"Good morning," Faith said as she poked her head up from the refrigerator.

Callie's heart pounded knowing she was caught trying to sneak out. She immediately began thinking for something to clever to say.

"Good morning to you," she answered in a high pitch she immediately knew sounded fake. "You're up early."

Faith smiled and nodded out through the glass sliders to the rocking chairs. Rachel and Maya were sitting quietly, paging through their phones while enjoying large cups of coffee.

"We're all early risers," Faith added almost apologetically.

"So, I see," Callie answered thinking her husband and kids would still be in bed until after nine.

"We were trying to stay quiet so you could sleep. I guess we failed."

The smell of coffee pulled Callie to the carafe that had just finished filling. Jason's carefully placed mug she used in the fall with *Raddest Dad* on its side was front and center on the counter. To not give them something to laugh about later, Callie reached past that mug to choose a blue generic one that hosted the North Carolina flag.

As Faith, Callie and Molly exited out of the air conditioning into the hot, moist beach air, Rachel and Maya stopped their conversation to assess Callie's condition and whether she had any lingering effects of the cocktail flu so early in the morning. To their eyes, Callie seemed fine and unaffected by the mix of drinks she had the night before.

"I want you to know that I really appreciate you being so nice to me last night, and for offering me a bed to sleep in."

"Anytime," each replied.

"I think I'm going to head back to Williamsburg as soon as my head clears a little and this coffee kicks in."

The girls all shared glances as they watched Callie position for her exit. After finishing her cup through some light conversation, Callie let Molly run on the beach one last time then revisited the bathroom herself before grabbing her bag to walk down to her car.

The three girls walked with her and Molly to be polite and to send her on her way. It was an expectation they knew their dad would want them to do. The light chatter between them ended abruptly as they descended the stairs to see the Black Range Rover HSE parked in the driveway. Rachel's initial reaction was to heave then hold a belly laugh while shaking her head in disbelief. That Callie drove the exact, same car as their mom after she divorced their dad was too much to handle so early in the morning. Callie loaded her bag into the back of the car then put Molly into her usual driver seat spot before returning to say good-bye with a hug for each of them.

As the Range Rover backed onto the street, Maya had to share a thought through clenched lips.

"Does anyone else find it hysterical that she has the exact, same car as mom?"

Callie turned the wheel then tooted the horn as she pulled away to proceed down the street. A burst of laughter erupted from the girls as the car disappeared back into houses.

"She's heading to Asheville," Maya said with her eyes still fixated on where Callie turned. "I told her where dad is."

"That's cool," Faith added giving approval.

"I don't like her," Rachel grumbled before turning to walk back to the house. "I mean, for dad."

# # # #

The GPS' ETA at Fox Farm a little after four o'clock. The drive was a straight shot of highway across the state of North Carolina through Raleigh/Durham and Statesville before heading off into the mountains. Callie felt guilty about misleading Jason's girls about where she was heading. But she was also afraid that if she told them that one would call him to give advance warning that she was on her way. Callie still wanted their reunion to be a surprise.

As she passed Raleigh, Callie noted the signs for NC State where Maya was in school. She began thinking how the drive was so easy; and why Maya was a regular at the beach in the fall. Her visits likely did not change when winter cold turned to the spring and warmer days. The cities and towns that followed became less exciting as the grind of the drive set in through Winston-Salem, Statesville and up to Hickory.

As Callie re-entered the interstate after a pit stop for gas, refreshment and a bathroom visit, her Spotify mood music cutout to be replaced by an Ariana Grande ringtone she assigned to her daughter Lizzie. Lizzie was her youngest of three children and a year younger than Maya. The song choice made Callie always think of Lizzie. She was happy to hear from her daughter to break up the otherwise boring drive.

"Hi sweetie," Callie answered excited to talk.

"MOM, can I come home!?" Lizzie asked loudly without even a hello.

"Why!? What's wrong?"

"It sucks here. I don't have anyone to hang with. And, Dad is paying attention to some southern bimbo that's staying at a BNB on the island."

Callie's immediate thought was that Chase manipulated their family vacation to invite the lover he said he dumped to be in Nantucket with him. The complete disregard for his children's psyche and fun infuriated her. The disrespect he was showing for her in front of their "friends" and his family took her emotions to a boil.

"Let me get this straight?" Callie asked. "Your father has a woman with him on the island?"

"Not really. I don't know," Lizzie answered. "He did go out with friends last night and came back really early this morning. His car is so loud and woke me up."

"Jesus Christ, Chase," Callie whispered in anger. "Honey, it'll be fine. You'll be fine,"

Callie elevated her voice to be heard.

"Where are you?" Lizzie interrupted.

The question haunted Callie with the memory from the fall when that same question resulted in the first direct lie she had ever told any of her children.

"I'm in North Carolina heading to Asheville."

"I love Asheville," Lizzie replied. "The Biltmore. The shoppes. The fooood. Can I fly there and catch up with you?"

Callie muted her phone to scream at the windshield. Her two youngest kids were not excited about going to Nantucket with their dad in July. Their usual vacation was in August when the water and winds were warmer. That he was spending time with his *home wrecking whore* of a girlfriend instead of with his kids and family showed a total disregard for them. After regaining her calm, Callie unmuted the phone.

"I'm sorry honey. I must have hit a dead zone."

The other end of the line remained quiet as Callie listened for signs of Lizzie.

"It's OK mom," Lizzie replied. "So, can I come visit you?"

The distraction of the call, which was supposed to be a good thing, put her driving on autopilot. As she became angry, her speed increased to over ninety miles per hour in a seventy zone. The flashing blue North Carolina Highway Patrol lights that reflected in her rearview mirror startled her back to real time thought.

"Oh great," Callie muttered. "Lizzie, sweetie, I have to go,"

Callie signaled then pulled far off onto the berm to give the patrolman plenty of room hoping that may be appreciated with just a warning.

"So, I can come?" Lizzie answered in excitement.

"No, sweetie," Callie answered now stopped and waiting patiently for the patrolman to visit her door. "I have to go."

Callie abruptly hung up the phone through her steering wheel then quickly checked her hair and make-up in the mirror. She was hopeful the car and her looks would help her talk her way out of the ticket. As she pondered some excuses, none sounded strong enough to sell. So, she decided to be honest and vent her marital frustrations to the patrolman who was slowly approaching.

After providing all the documents the patrolman requested, his single question of her knowing how fast she was going received a two-minute dissertation on her husband's infidelity and current whoring in Nantucket. The tears she shed out of anger were read as emotional distress persuading the officer to give her a warning and to send her on her way.

As she merged back into traffic, Callie decided she needed time to recover from both Lizzie's call and being pulled over for speeding. She declared no more phone calls for the remainder of the trip.

# # # #

Since his arrival, a fallen tree by the man-made, lily pond in front of Fox Farm's main house bothered Jason. The bulk of the tree landed over the pond's spillway and, over time, had collected enough leaves, silt, and debris to completely block water from escaping. With continued feed from the natural springs on the property, the pond's water level was rising and encroaching on the property's main driveway. Jason's initial hope was that the rising water level would create enough pressure to push the debris through enabling the pond to drain back down to normal. But now that the water was nearing the gravel drive, he decided it was time to make an intervention.

The spillway sat on the south end of the pond and measured over twenty feet across. The pond had a traditional clay floor with a four-foot mounded lip to both dam the water and to give immediate depth. The natural clay in the area worked well for holding water. It did not erode easily; and, water did not permeate through it. The spillway was framed on both sides by thick shrubs that grew back into the tree line.

Jason grabbed a chainsaw and a shovel from the supply shed before walking down to assess the problem. Zoe tagged along excited to be near the main house and pond. She always loved to walk the property and to take a swim.

Clara saw the two stroll by as she was finishing dishes from the brunch pick-up. Although she had complete confidence in her husband Tom, who could work magic with a chainsaw, she shook her head in disbelief and concern as she watched Jason heading out with Tom's saw and shovel.

The temptation to offer to help nagged her as she watched Jason survey the job. He motioned his right hand in karate chop fashion as he envisioned the cuts he would make and the resulting fall of wood from the from the tree. He seemed to be debating several approaches when finally coming upon one he felt would work. His focus and motions appeared to favor the other side of the spillway where the bottom of the tree was located.

Zoe sat quietly next to him with a stick then waded into the water as Jason ignored her. He then began to climb out on the tree with the chainsaw instead of walking around the pond to complete his desired cut. As each moment passed, Clara became more nervous for his safety. The footing was visibly sketchy as he struggled to hold the chainsaw in his left hand while grabbing tree limbs with his right. The looming accident she saw building could not be ignored. She toweled her hands dry to go help.

"Do you need some help!?" Clara shouted as she strutted quickly down through the grass.

As Jason looked up to see her coming, his foot slipped from the perch he was holding causing him to tense with panic. Although not large, the tree had limbs that were thick enough to support his weight as he slowly journeyed out over the water. The slip jammed his right foot into a cluster of limbs below. He fought to hold his composure as the pain of the contact and resulting scrapes shot through his body. Regardless of how much it hurt, he was not letting go of the tree limb to fall and lose the chainsaw in the water.

"Are you OK?" Clara asked as she stopped by the side of the spillway.

"I'm fine," he mumbled, embarrassed that he was now stuck in the tree half-way over the spillway. "I had an idea that's not going to work."

"Well, please be careful."

Jason paused for a moment to give her a look that showed contempt despite also being meant to instill confidence. Each step he took was beginning to bounce the tree trunk like a trampoline. Clara was noticeably nervous about his dangerous approach to solve the farm's spillway problem. As he methodically stepped to make his way back to shore, Clara moved to the waterline to take the chainsaw from him. Without it, Jason could finish his tree trek safely with two hands and without the burden of a heavy, sharp power tool.

Jason had a few more steps through the top of the tree where the branches were less cumbersome but also weaker. Because of the dam, he was still positioned over the four feet of black, murky water that sat in front of the spillway. He stopped to steady his balance as Clara tensed with each movement he made.

6

Callie was happy to finally be on Blackridge Road. It was the final leg of the drive to the Fox Farm. Her GPS had her destination a mile and a half down the road and on the right. The forest on both sides was dense. She hoped the entrance to the farm was going to show to be more than a dirt drive back into the weeds. She wanted to see it early enough to turn rather than drive by it.

As the arrow that marked her position on the dashboard display map closed in on her destination, the forest on the right opened to a field that hosted a split rail wood fence lining the road to two stone pillars each with a wrought iron gate. A sign identifying Fox Farm hung from a wood post with matching wrought iron hangers. Callie looked at the farm's sign with a critical thought on the its logo design.

As she made the turn onto the stone driveway, Callie was impressed with manicured property that surrounded the freshly painted historic home that sat a hundred yards away. On her drive up the main drive, she noticed small directional signs pointing down narrow lanes off into the trees. The cabins all had strong names. The first lane lead to Iron Eagle and Stoneridge. The second lane to Flying Dutchman and Swiss Chalet. Looking beyond the house, Callie could see similar paths leading off that had signs that were too small to read. The property was proving to be more intriguing than she expected. She was anxious to find Jason to both surprise him and to tour Fox Farm and the area for as long as he was there.

The parking area to the main house had room for eight cars before needing to use the grass. A front walk led from the gravel lot up to the front porch filled with rockers from end to end. After she parked her Range Rover near the stairs, Callie clipped Molly's leash back on to her collar before exiting. Having slept through the entire trip, Molly was anxious to get her legs moving. She eagerly bounded over the center console and jumped down to the ground to explore with Callie. Together, they walked to the main office hoping to either be directed to Jason or announced.

# # # #

Clara heard the car noise and noticed the arrival of the unexpected black Range Rover as she anxiously waited to grab the chainsaw. Jason still had a few steps across the tree before reaching solid ground. Having quickly left the kitchen, Clara did not think to leave a note on the front counter that she was on property and would be right back. Clara knew Jason had to rid himself of the chainsaw before taking his final steps toward shore. As he paused to study his next step and path, Clara shifted her eyes to see the fit, middle-aged woman with obvious means walk up to and into the house.

"Jason. Someone just arrived," Clara said, anxious to get him moving.

"Just go. I'll be fine. I've got like five steps left to get off this thing."

Clara agreed with his count but not with his confidence he could do it alone. She had watched his feet move from branch to branch. Each new foothold was giving less support and grip to keep him out of the water. As he worked his way closer to her, Clara leaned out over the waterline to offer her hand.

"Hand me the chain saw," she urged reaching out as far as she could while he was setting his foot to a secure his balance.

"It's heavy," he answered. "I've got it."

"Just hand me the damn thing!" Clara demanded in a combined frustrated laugh and whisper.

She was mentally counting the time that had passed since the woman walked into the office.

"OK," he answered. "Hold on. Here it comes."

Jason steadied his balance as he brought his hands together. He had to transfer the chainsaw from his waterside left hand to his right that was stronger and nearer to Clara. Clara took another step closer and had one foot sitting at the edge of the over-flow water near the spillways drop-off into the deeper water. Her footing on the silt on top of the clay was uncertain as she stretched out her right arm to take the saw.

As Jason shifted and reached to her, the transfer of the saw from his to her hands was successful. But as he started to let go, the weight was too much for Clara's extended reach and her arms dropped abruptly. To keep from losing the saw into the water, Jason stretched to grab the saw and to help her.

The crack of the tree limb shot across the open, grassy area and into the house. Although the trunk of the tree did not snap completely, it was bent and twisted toward the water shift-ing Jason's weight precariously forward. Callie heard the loud, sharp noise as she gave up on finding anyone in the main house and exited back onto its front porch. Nervous laughter erupted from the pond that pulled her attention toward the spillway, Jason, Clara, and the chainsaw.

Jason's body dropped down again as a second crack sounded. The sounds that followed were loud gasps as Jason slipped again dropping him into the water and pulling the woman who was helping in with him.

Callie's immediate impulse was to run toward them to offer help. Although there was nothing she could do, she wanted to make sure both were OK.

As he surfaced, Jason was covered in pieces of organic matter that littered his face and salt-n-pepper hair. Because of her face-forward, belly-flop entry, Clara was also soaked but managed to keep her face, and most of her hair, out of the water. The chainsaw disappeared somewhere into water and silt that was around them.

Jason stood and cleared his face as he looked at Clara who was picking wet leaves of her Fox Farm tee-shirt. The shirt's usually loose heavy cotton was stuck to her body giving him a good look at her physique. As she dropped the final leaf back into the water, Clara looked to Jason to check his disposition. His face lacked expression. Jason was also concerned that she may be mad at him for pulling her into the nasty water. What she found was that his expression was notably absent of any embarrassment that his stupidity caused them both to take an unexpected plunge into the pond. Both started to laugh as they looked at the other covered in pond scum.

As Callie slowly moved toward the pond, she took a few abrupt steps then paused to watch the two in the water. It was comforting for her to see Jason taking the fall into the nasty water so well. Chase would have been livid and blamed her had Callie been Clara.

The slick silt that covered clay bottom was proving more slippery than Jason had anticipated. As he stepped to offer Clara his hand to escort her back out of the pond, his plant foot slipped throwing him off balance. After a flurry of anxious arm swings, he disappeared back under the murky water again.

Clara waited for Jason to reappear and saw neither him nor any bubbles. When he slowly did reappear from the darkness, his resurface stopped just as his closed eyes cleared the waterline. Clara began to laugh as he opened them then paused.

"Don't even think about it," she warned as she raised her hand in defense.

Jason slowly lifted his clenched hands in front of his face to shoot a wicked stream of water at her as he again submerged. Clara's instinct to turn her face and close her eyes did little to save her from the spray of water. Feeling calm after minimizing his assault, she looked back for him to find no one.

The tight grab on both ankles was haunting; and, she screamed as she disappeared into the murky water. As she quickly re-emerged in a burst, she shook her arms, head, and hair to separate them from the nasty water debris. Jason rose slowly again keeping eyes just over the waterline to survey the situation. As he stood, he laughed as Clara continued to flap her arms in disgust with the pond scum that dripped from her.

"You wear it well," he joked while grabbing her hand and splashing more water at her.

"I can't believe you just did that to me," Clara answered in disguised laughter as she swatted water back at him. "There's someone waiting up in the office."

"No," Callie answered. "She came down to see if you two needed help. Which you obviously do NOT."

Jason immediately dropped Clara's hand as he locked eyes with Callie. His heart sank as he heard the disdain in her voice as she stood within a stone's throw of where he was frolicking with another woman. The image of Jason and Clara playing in the mud immediately sent the message of *couple* through Callie's mind. That woman had to be why Jason went silent on Facebook; and, also why he was so secretive about his trips to Asheville.

Callie recognized the woman in the pond as the wife of the farm's owner which had to have an entirely separate story. But given her own year-to-date trauma and the drama of the day, the compounding pressure grew to be too much for Callie to process and to handle. After a short, silent glare, she stormed back toward her car as Jason struggled to exit the water.

"Callie, wait!" he shouted as he struggled to move on the pond's slippery bottom.

But, by the time he was out and had helped Clara back onto to the grass, Callie had reached the parking area. After several more ignored calls from him, the Range Rover was back on Blackburn Road roaring back toward Virginia.

# # # #

It took a few minutes for Jason to get to the shed where he left his phone. This gave Callie plenty of time to put distance between them, think about, and misinterpret what she had just witnessed. How Callie had found him at Fox Farm, seven hours away from his cottage at the beach, added to his intrigue. One of his girls must have told her that he was there without the courtesy of a heads-up that she was coming. That could only mean that she visited the cottage looking for him.

Clara gave him a pat on the shoulder for support as she passed to head back to the main house to shower and change. The anger she would have had for being pulled into the pond had been replaced by the joy of playfully flirting with the man she always found inteesting and was beginning to find attractive. The woman that appeared at the side of the pond was an unknown to her. But it was clear to Clara that she was competition for her to win Jason regardless if Clara was competition for her.

As he used an old rag to clean his hands of pond residue, Jason tried to launch his iPhone. The facial identification was not cooperating because of the debris on his face and in his wretched hair. He used his voice activation to make the call.

"Hey Siri, call Callie Larson."

The history they shared both twenty-eight years ago, and more recently last October, gave Jason the understanding that, when mad, Callie does not answer her phone. Her initial storm-out and acceleration out of the driveway and down the road was a strong indication that she was likely still very angry and hurt.

It also meant that her phone was still likely in her purse. Even with Bluetooth connectivity in her Range Rover, Jason knew that Callie would not answer his call. But he had to call before texting.

Please come back.

The message appeared on the screen on her dashboard accompanied by a phone ding that broke the silence in her car. Jason's belief that Callie was still gunning down Blackburn Road to the interstate heading home was wrong. After getting out of sight of the property, Callie found a pull-off where it was safe to park, breath, and breakdown completely. Her broken life that was showing rays of renewal through her rediscovery of Jason Cartwright appeared to be going dark again.

# # # #

Clara knew to ask Jason anything as he walked past the kitchen back to the Flying Dutchman was not going to be helpful. Through her time knowing him, he openly talked about his careers, his family, kids, and life that were positive or related, in some way, to Fox Farm.

As she stood in the mudroom of the main house, the smell from the pond that attached to her started to become pungent as her adrenalin high waned. With meals due to arrive soon, Clara watched Jason walk back to his cabin holding his cell phone in hand. When he finally made the turn down the wooded lane and disappeared into the trees, Clara rushed off to shower and change. Her head, however, would not reorient from the pretty, rich woman she just about met. Someone who was obviously significant to Jason while also now troubling to her.

7

Callie stared with teary, blurred vision at Jason's message as it hung on her screen. Her exhaustion was crippling. She had no energy to move. No energy to drive. And, most of all, no energy to deal with Jason Cartwright's explanation of his antics with the wife of the couple that owned the property where he was staying. Why and how he ended up in the pond with that woman did matter as she rehashed the playful frolic between the two in the disgusting water.

Callie looked to Molly who was waiting patiently in the seat next to hers. Without call, Molly jumped into Callie's lap to give her comfort.

"You're the only one who doesn't disappoint me," Callie admitted to the dog as she hugged her tightly. "The only one I can count on."

After one last hug, Callie directed Molly back to her seat. She gave her a pat on her head as Molly sat upright expecting a treat. With a stash in the center console, Callie fed one treat to Molly then offered her a second. After swallowing her reward, and noting the bag heading back in the console, Molly curled back in a ball to continue the road trip.

Watching Molly go from cuddle back to sleep calmed Callie as she pulled back out on to the road. The woods that bordered the two lanes ahead of her extended out then curved off into the forest as Callie felt her truck accelerate through its gears. As she turned the corner, the same view repeated with the same scenery. The road that traveled so quickly on the way in seemed to be going on forever on the way out.

When Callie arrived at the interstate, she was happy to see a road that offered a faster escape. But as she slowed, she found herself presented with a dilemma. She could travel west to Asheville to find a place to stay for the night to give her time to think. Or, she could travel east back toward the coast, Williamsburg, or even back to D.C. She knew to drive back to Williamsburg would get her there after midnight. And Asheville, despite all its food and fun venues, was not going to be fun by herself. She fought the desire to go somewhere other than back to Fox Farm. But she knew that she had to resolve what she had driven so far to find before leaving it behind again, for good.

# # # #

Clara stood wearing clean clothes and brushed wet hair as she prepared baskets that would host the food that was due to arrive. Her practice was to prepare twelve baskets each night to be sure she was able to quickly transfer and deliver the meals as they arrived. Since each meal was ordered directly from its source to ensure timely delivery and accuracy, Clara was never sure exactly how many deliveries she would have to make. Six was always the expectation as guests would leave to visit Asheville and the Lake Lure restaurants. The basket presentation was a feature Jason felt Clara should hire helpers to effect faster transfer and delivery to the cabins. But, up until Jason, that option was not an option because more staff would have required paying more wages the property could not afford.

Clara was behind with her basket preparation after taking the time to completely de-louse from her unplanned swim in the pond. The small pieces of debris that stuck to every exposed part of her body were particularly obstinate to remove from her hair, ears, and nose. As she showered aggressively to remove every, last piece of pond from her body, her recall of Jason's tree-walk, stumble, and fall into the water, that also resulted in her being pulled in with him, gave her pause to laugh. That happening, along with his playful re-dunk and splashing, was the first pure joy she had felt since before her husband passed-away. As she prepared the final baskets, she reveled in another mental replay of his fall and her swim.

"Stop it Clara," she said quietly to herself. "Stop thinking about that."

As Clara closed the lid on the final basket, she looked down the line of neatly prepared, elegant food containers ready for action. She was satisfied that the row of wicker was ready for the food that was about to arrive. As she stood admiring her work, the front doorbell jingled to let her know someone had arrived. Expecting it was one of her food vendors, she walked through the dining room to greet them in the front hall.

"I'd really appreciate you using the kitchen door," Clara said in advance of her seeing who it was. "It's easier to bring the meals in for trans…ferrrr."

Clara's tone dropped off quickly as what she expected to be a delivery man appeared as the nicely dressed, early fifties woman that stormed away after witnessing the pond play.

"Hello," Clara said sheepishly with a slight laugh. "I'm so sorry. I thought you were a delivery man."

Callie stepped forward as Clara entered the room to greet her. Her demeanor was cautious as she looked around the room with a blank expression. She then clutched her purse as she stepped to the counter.

"Hi," she replied exhausting air to calm herself. "I'm looking for Jason Cartwright. Can you tell me where I can find him?"

Clara's heart started pounding as she had two simultaneous thoughts. The first was a wonder of who this woman in front of her was who stunned Jason then ran when she saw their pond play. Her second thought was jealousy that was beginning to erupt while looking directly at her apparent competition. Competition she did not know existed until earlier that day.

"Well, I know you saw him here earlier. So, I won't ask you the usual questions to protect his privacy." Clara answered with a slight rudeness in her voice.

Callie chose not to respond to Clara's declaration. Instead she just raised her eyebrows to again ask to be directed to Jason.

"I can call his cabin to see if he'll see you," Clara offered. "Or you can text him on his cell phone; and he can give you directions. I hope you understand that I just can't send you there unannounced."

Callie understood the words Clara was saying as she felt her heart sink. The magical surprise she envisioned at the beach, and then at Fox Farm, was being ruined by a pond frolic and property policy to not give directions blindly to unfamiliar people who show up looking for guests.

"This was supposed to be a surprise," Callie mumbled in frustration.

"I can assure you it was," Clara offered feeling some empathy for the woman. "I can call back."

"No, I'll just text him. Thank you?"

Callie's elevated, questioning tone sought an introduction without either asking or offering her name.

"Clara," Clara responded. "I'm the property manager."

"Callie," Callie replied with a hesitant smile. "I'm the ex-fiancée from thirty years ago with really bad timing."

Callie abruptly turned as she finished her comment. There was nothing more to say. It was becoming obvious to her that Jason's continued travels back and forth to Fox Farm was to see the beautiful woman she had just met. One of two owners who were married to each other as of the last publishing of the website. A status that Callie knew, from personal experience, could change quickly long before the spouse discovers it and a website can be updated.

Clara's immediate inclination was to call Jason. But her inner voice told her that Callie's apparent frustration would likely lead her to leave the property if she did not immediately try to text him. What Callie said, and how she said it, gave Clara a strong impression of who Callie was and why Jason reacted the way he did. The fast start of her car and its immediate drive toward the road gave Clara hope that Callie was leaving. As she watched the Range Rover barrel by the lane back to the *Flying Dutchman*, she felt relief that her initial thoughts were right.

"Callie!" Jason yelled as he ran out from the lane to chase the Range Rover.

Clara repositioned to watch Callie's brake lights illuminate as dust kicked up from her skidding tires on the gravel. Clara moved closer to the door to listen and for a better view as Jason sprinted to the driver side of the car. Callie stayed in her car as its motor continued to run and her brake lights continued to glow. After what looked like a few tense comments, the brake lights went out, the exhaust out the back stopped, and Jason opened the door to help Callie out for a long, emotional hug. Clara backed silently into the shadow of the door as she watched a reunion she did not think was going to happen. And, for the first time since Tom's death, her heart felt broken again.

As she watched Jason hold the door for Callie to get back into her car, Clara felt her stomach ache as he pointed to and down the road to the *Flying Dutchman.* Callie backed her car to give her access to the road. She then stopped briefly as she pulled forward to let Jason climb clumsily into the passenger seat as Molly was directed to the back seat. The black SUV then disappeared into the thick summer foliage after stirring a trace of dust that soon settled back down behind it.

8

The weather on Nantucket was gray and cool due a constant easterly wind that blew the sand and bent the dune grass toward the North Atlantic. After talking to her mom, Lizzie decided to spend the day in her room looking out over the sweatshirt clad brave hearts who were sitting on the beach with coolers as others dared to swim in the water. Lizzie kept her phone handy to scan posts and to communicate with her friends back in Virginia. Her dad disappeared again after taking a morning nap and eating a quick lunch by himself. He left cash for her and her brother Will to either order dinner to be delivered or to venture out in an Uber to find something they wanted. Will decided to take half the money and find dinner on his own with his friends leaving Lizzie home and alone to fend for herself.

The end of her conversation with her mother earlier in the afternoon did not give Lizzie hope that Callie would want to talk again. Her mother would just advocate staying in Nantucket because she and Lizzie loved Nantucket. But what was missing this year for Lizzie was Callie. Callie and Lizzie would buddy-up over these vacations as the boys would run to either do things together or with their dad. Callie being absent this year had a double impact of a friend being missing and her mom being gone.

To fill time, Lizzie decided to Facetime her grandmother, Carolyn. Carolyn, Callie's mother, lived in Williamsburg that was a few hours' drive from both Washington and the Outer Banks. Carolyn was a typical grandmother. She was not tech savvy and struggled with each new gadget she would get. But after Lizzie's brothers showed their Gram Facetime on her iPod, she began using it regularly to reach out to her family that was now scattered across several states and one ocean. The trick, they found, for reaching Carolyn, was simple timing. Many times, the first few call attempts would time-out requiring immediate redials so that Gram could find her iPod and activate its Facetime app.

The initial image that appeared on Lizzie's phone was the ceiling fan in Carolyn's kitchen. A jostling followed then blurred until it finally rested framing Carolyn and the view from her kitchen into her sunroom.

"Hi kiddo," Carolyn opened happy to see Lizzie on her screen.

"Hi Grammy," Lizzie answered. "How are things today in Williamsburg?"

Carolyn's video was choppy and periodically froze as the call settled into her internet service. The contortions of her face and misaligned sound were often laughs that Callie and Lizzie would secretly screenshot and share.

"Things are hot and quiet here sweetie. Just the way Gram likes them. How are things at home?"

Lizzie was puzzled by the question then looked behind her to see what backdrop Carolyn saw that would make her think Lizzie was home.

"Gram," she said. "We're in Nantucket."

Embarrassed about forgetting, Carolyn's eyes widened as she realized her mistake. With Callie visiting up until the day before, and now nowhere to be seen since, it was difficult for her to think of Callie's family in Nantucket without her.

"I'm sorry honey, Gram's just a little confused on where you all are."

"Dad, Will, and I are in Nantucket. Michael is in Spain. Mom is somewhere in the North Carolina mountains, I think. But she hung up on me really fast. I don't know why."

Carolyn remained still as if lost in thought. She then returned when she heard Lizzie mention Chase. Although Nantucket was his family's vacation spot for generations, the past twenty-five years he went there was with Callie, and the kids. That, by itself, should have been enough to take at least a year off through the divorce.

"Was she upset?" Carolyn asked thinking Callie said she was going to the beach to visit Jason.

"No, well, yes," Lizzie explained. "She was happy to talk until I told her I wasn't having any fun this year."

Carolyn's heart sank for her only granddaughter. Lizzie was a quiet, sensitive child that Callie protected almost to a fault. She knew the two were kindred spirits on Nantucket Island and did everything together. The double whammy of the divorce happening, and Callie not being there as Lizzie's island friend, was a lot for the nineteen-year-old to deal with.

"She'd certainly understand why you're blue, sweetie. What else happened?"

"Well, she said she was going to Asheville which is this really cool city in the North Carolina mountains."

"Asheville?" Carolyn qualified.

Carolyn thought for a moment unable to think of anything that would pull Callie there. Jason lived at the beach.

"Yes," Lizzie answered. "I asked if I could fly to catch up to her; and, she just cut me off. Said 'NO!'"

Carolyn's mind was busy running Asheville as Lizzie continued to speak. She was looking for any reason why Callie would head to the mountains when the person she wanted to see lived on the ocean just two hours away.

"That would be an expensive flight," Carolyn stated just to reply. "It'd be difficult with connections in New York, maybe

Charlotte."

"Gram, I've flown before. It's no big deal."

The condescension in Lizzie's voice amused her grandmother. *Atta girl* for the can-do adventurous spirit was her first thought. Her grandfather would have been proud to hear it if he was still alive.

"Well, I'm sure your mother had her reasons. What's your dad say?"

Carolyn's shoulders cringed then radiated down through her back as she pictured a conversation between Lizzie and Chase.

"Grammy, he doesn't care. He'd probably prefer it since he's flirting around with some forty-year-old bimbo who's staying nearby."

Lizzie's words shifted Carolyn's demeanor from a happy, inquisitive to angry.

"Did you share that with your mother?"

The question was answered by Lizzie's blank expression on the screen and silence.

"I couldn't lie to her," she admitted softly.

Lizzie's expression shifted to guilt for her action as Carolyn sat back on her stool.

"No, sweetie, No. You certainly couldn't," Carolyn gasped.

Carolyn knew Callie would be extremely angered by Chase hosting any woman other than her on their family's first vacation since the divorce started. Her expectation was that the affair he said he ended never ended, or, at least, had rekindled since he moved out in February. Chase with another woman in Nantucket effectively obliterated any hope that he and Callie would find their ways back together. The promise they made to each other and to God on their wedding day was staying broken.

"Sweetie, it will all be fine. Let me call your mom to see what I can do."

Lizzie's face lit with excitement knowing the influence Carolyn had on Callie.

"And," Carolyn added. "If that can't happen... you can certainly come visit me instead."

Carolyn smirked knowing her second offer had no appeal to her granddaughter. Visiting Gram in Williamsburg did not trump loneliness in Nantucket. She knew Lizzie would decide to stay if her only choices were there or Williamsburg. But catching up with Callie in Asheville may just offer Lizzie the comfort she needed as her father galivanted around in front of her and her brother with a younger woman.

"Thanks Gram," Lizzie closed hopeful that her grandmother's influence to make Asheville happen would work.

The two exchanged smiles and finished with a touch-to-lips then touch-to-screen gesture before signing off. Lizzie began to feel hope that the pain of her vacation in Nantucket would soon be over. Carolyn pondered how she would approach Callie with both questions that needed answered and the suggestion she fly Lizzie to Asheville to get away from Chase.

# # # #

The drive back to the cabin was silent. Jason knew Callie was still thinking about what she saw at the pond. He also knew he had things to work out personally because of how his relationship with Clara was evolving. He used a few words to direct the turns but otherwise kept from saying anything else.

As the Range Rover drove up and over the small hill that dropped down to the *Flying Dutchman*, Callie was impressed by the cabin's design and presence as it sat extended out over the hillside. The entrance was clean, simple, and attractive. There were two empty parking spots by the front door. Fox Farm was far nicer than what she expected when she first saw the pictures on the website.

"Don't you have a car here?" Callie asked noting no car in sight. "How'd you get here?"

Callie's follow-up question had a nervous element to it. Her voice elevated as she turned to Jason with piercing eyes to get a simple answer.

"It's back at the main house," Jason said with a slight laugh. "I'm letting Clara…. the property manager…. use it while the farm's Jeep is in the shop."

The qualification of Clara as the property manager slipped by Callie again. There was no relief for her in his answer. It only raised a question of why he, as a guest, would lend his car or truck to the property owner. She also wondered where Clara's husband from the website was. The entire situation became more confusing as she continued to think about it. But she also knew that she would get answers in time. And, given the stresses of the day and her bad "surprise" reconnection with him already, the fact that he chased her down this time then invited her back to his cottage was a turning point. She was now with him in his cabin which added comfort. The competitive thoughts of who Clara was to him were fading.

As Jason grabbed her suitcase from her car, Molly ran with Zoe outside while Callie continued to study her new environment. The cabin that presented a rustic footprint at first impression was showing to have nice and refined finishes. Her nerves that were jagged until now continued to settle as she began to feel relaxed and continued to survey the setting.

"Got any wine?" she asked him as he wheeled her bag into the front hall.

# # # #

Jason had made eight o'clock reservations at the Lakeside Inn on Lake Lure as soon as it opened for lunch at 11 AM. The dinner was intended to be a *thank you* to Clara for their long-overdue dinner the night before. His plan was to invite her as a late afternoon *thought* that he could magically pull-off as a last-minute effort to secure one of the hardest-to-get tables by the water. In hindsight, it was fortunate that their unexpected swim in the lily pond disrupted his thinking and plans given Callie's unexpected arrival.

After Callie left his beach cottage with Chase in October, she was all he thought about as he looked for things to fill his time through the winter, spring, and early summer. Clara's appeal and warmth were becoming an unexpected attraction that was both subtly growing and exciting. Her influence made him re-think his *ONE* theory after Callie's long winter, spring, and early summer silence. He began to see her non-communication after her Thanksgiving Day text asking him *to wait for her* meant that she was not coming back. He was getting ready to set sail to move on.

Callie packed an array of clothes that covered beach casual and Williamsburg elegant. The *Flying Dutchman* was a two-bedroom cabin with two bathrooms. To not give Jason immediate expectations, Callie wheeled her suitcase into the guestroom. It was the first time since her break with Chase that her excitement to be with Jason made her extremely nervous.

Callie struggled to choose an outfit to wear. Although Lake Lure hosted a cluster of wealth from surrounding cities, she hesitated not wanting to be either too city sophisticated or casual for the night. She looked through her cracked door to see Jason pass by dressed for the night. Her confidence grew as she aligned his dress level to her desires and expectations.

Jason felt a need to calm and walked toward the cottage's small bar. He was dressed in Birkenstock sandals, pressed off-white linen pants and an open collared blue shirt. The reservation he made requested the deck overlooking the water instead of inside in the frigid air-conditioning that he was finding more and more uncomfortable.

Jason respectfully knocked on Callie's door to deliver her first wine that she called her *dresser* when they were dating and engaged. She was in the bathroom finishing her makeup when Jason set her *dresser* on her dresser.

Jason knew Callie would need time to get ready and returned to prepare his first drink of the evening. It was a double Roughrider bourbon whisky, neat. It was to both calm his nerves and to give him some inner strength to hear her news from the last nine months.

Jason walked outside for some air and was standing by the rail overlooking the woods when he heard the screen door slide. A smile came to his face as he turned to see Callie step through the doorway adorned in an elegant, green, open-shoulder silk dress she knew he would love. The dress was complemented by a light shawl in case they were near air-conditioning.

Jason smiled as their eyes met. His admiration and head-to-toe scan of her brought back memories from October when she first admitted to herself feeling love for him again. His look, that showed complete adoration, compelled Callie to spin and giggle as she walked toward him. As she took her last step, she leaned against him as she commandeered his glass of bourbon, finished it, then stretched upward on her toes to kiss him lightly on the lips. Her desire was for them to pick-up where they left off in October. The high Jason was enjoying from Callie's presence, look, strut and bourbon-laced kiss made the world evaporate around her.

"You look amazing," he said.

"Ditto," she replied with an upward glance and smile.

Jason gave a quick glance to his watch to check the time to decide on how to stage the evening. The time read ten minutes before seven. He knew the drive to Lake Lure would take about fifteen minutes. Maybe a little bit longer if he took the scenic route. They had some time to kill.

"Let's go," he said as he smiled and extended his hand for hers.

Molly and Zoe stood as they left the deck and followed their parents to the front door. Anxious to go, they were disappointed when the door closed in front of them. As they returned back to their chosen sleeping spot, both checked their bowls for food and to take a drink before settling in until their parents returned home.

# # # #

Clara was about halfway through her normal ritual of sweeping the front porch when the Black Range Rover appeared from out of the trees. From a distance, she could see that Jason was driving. He was dressed to go out; and Callie was with him in the passenger seat. Desite trying, Clara was having trouble shaking the animosity that erupted when Callie returned to interrupt her time with Jason. She stepped back into the shadows to not add stress to their situation by being seen. She was not surprised to see the SUV turn right to drive past the house up toward the upper property. She knew what Jason wanted to show her.

As her one hundred-thousand-dollar SUV slowly rocked heavily back and forth up the narrow, overgrown timber trail, Callie began to get nervous. Jason's focus stayed on his slow ascent through a severely rutted, washed-out area as Callie gave him looks of concern for her vehicle and herself. The road began to smooth again just as the woods cleared to a meadow. They had reached the top of the mountain.

The vista in front of her was nearly three hundred and sixty degrees of majestic, rich, blue sky that melded with the cotton ball clouds that flowed through it. The endless green of farmland below framed the bottom of her view with the mountains waffling throughout the middle. The surreal panorama in front of her was a stark difference from the view she used to covet in her Northern Virginia home. That vista of manicured lawns and like homes surrounded by endless apartment complexes, housing developments and shopping malls was losing its luster to this setting. The ride up the mountain reminded her of wood-lined drives she would take down along the Potomac into Georgetown just to get away from the sights of endless development around the capitol. Those roads made her nervous too.

The Range Rover came to a stop in the upper meadow giving a view that extended forever. As Jason shifted into Park, he leaned forward to look take it in as if for the first time.

"There should be a cabin here," Callie said as she shifted her eyes from the view to him.

Jason nodded his head in agreement as he just looked out the windshield.

"If you look down there," he said pointing down to the left. "There's a nice stream with a confluence that makes a nice swimming hole. Zoe loves it."

Callie looked down to see the whites of the water as it rushed beyond the trees. Her first thought was that a creek and pond with dogs would be an endless mess to deal with. But then she realized Jason had daily dealings with the sand Zoe would bring back to the cottage from the beach. From his play in the pond, any type of mess did not seem to bother him.

"This is beautiful. There should be a cabin right here," Callie repeated as if offering a great idea that was missed.

"Over through that gap in the trees," Jason added, "is direct access back out on to the road you drove in on. Comes out right by the main house pond."

Callie listened in disbelief as she wondered why he battered the undercarriage of her Range Rover when there was a gentler access through a meadow to the same destination?

"But it needs a bridge over the creek though," Jason finished knowing what she had been thinking having intentionally paused to enjoy taking her on more than one ride during this drive. "But I honestly think we could get through it with this thing."

Callie spun and looked at him in disbelief as she leaned to the windshield to look down the hill at the stream then back at the trail they forged through to get there.

"My car is NOT going through a creek!" she declared. "Now I know why there isn't a cabin up here."

"This is too nice for a cabin," Jason finally admitted with a smile. "This view deserves a house with lots of glass."

There were three remaining vistas that Clara and Tom Haigh had left unspoiled on the property because of limited resources and their indecision on where to build their own home. Jason gave Clara her pick of the three as part of his offer to buy Fox Farm. The lot was then separated and deeded to her to build on it as she wanted. After the closing, Tom's ashes were spread on her parcel just as he wanted when Clara was sure she was going to stay. Her parcel also was not Jason's first choice of the three which made the deal much easier for him moving forward.

Callie's stomach pitted with Jason's thinking and declaration. A house had more permanence than a cottage. His location at the beach was perfect. It was an easy two-hour drive to and from Williamsburg. And with her divorce processing and the house for sale, Callie expected that the obvious choice for her would be to first move to Williamsburg to support care for her aging mother as well as to give her a soft landing spot to re-established things with Jason at the beach.

Most of the cities from the Outer Banks up through Richmond offered the winter life and culture she would like when the ocean communities were empty. The thought of daily coffees on the cottage's beach overlook was romantic. The scenery in front of her, for as beautiful as it was, and as cool as she remembered Asheville to be, was at least six hours from her mom. This location would be more isolating and problematic for her to both date him and to attend to Carolyn's needs. But her fear calmed with knowing that to build his house there, Jason would have to buy the property then go through the process of designs, permits and construction. She had time to work him. It also did not seem that either Clara, or her husband, had any inclination or need to sell.

"This is spectacular," she finally pushed out as she gazed silently at a problem many wished they would have.

Jason just nodded agreement as he started the engine to start a second kidney-jarring ride back down the mountain. They had a lot to catch-up on, and even more to talk about.

9

The restaurant was small and nestled in the one hundred feet between the road and the lake. The deck where they were seated extended out over the water supported by posts that disappeared into the dark glimmer below. Citronella candles were lit and set on each railing post to provide a warm glow of light. The water added ambiance with a comforting lapping sound that blended with the murmur of conversations from the tables around them.

"So, you don't write or call me for nine months then decide it's OK to just show up without flowers,"

Jason voice was calm and sarcastic as he pushed Callie's chair to the table. He then kissed her cheek to complete his thought.

"Well, Jason Cartwright, you're not an easy man to find," she replied. "And, I wanted this to be a surprise."

"And you succeeded."

Jason laughed quietly as his eyes settled in on hers. Callie struggled to the hold eye contact with him then quickly looked away. She was now free to be with him if she wanted him; and that was suddenly making her uncomfortable. He was again with her, showing interest, and not being pulled away by some unknown dark demon like he was twenty-eight years ago. Callie felt her cheeks tighten as tears welled in her eyes. She kept her eyes away out over the water to not show her emotion.

"So, you went to the cottage first?" he asked to break the silence.

Callie wiped her mouth then attempted to dab her eyes to absorb the tears. When she looked at Jason, she knew they were bloodshot and swollen. There was no hiding her emotional state. She appreciated him redirecting the conversation to her journey rather than either her destination or starting point. Those conversations would come later.

"Yes," Callie answered. "My big plan after holding our AGREED silence was to surprise you yesterday. My kids are in Nantucket with their dad. I, of course, was NOT invited. So, I have two empty weeks while Will and Lizzie are there. So, after visiting with my mom for a day to get a pep talk... NOT. I went looking for you."

Callie was growing more comfortable with their eye contact. The expression on his face was attentive and appreciative of what she had to go through to both find and be with him. It was also cutting right through her. She took a drink of water to settle her nerves.

"You must have met my girls then?"

"I did," she answered, "and they're lovely. All three of them. Quite different from each other but played well together while I was there."

Jason was relieved to hear Callie was received and treated well. Her time with Maya in the fall showed him that Callie's personality fit well into his family's dynamic and mindset. But he also knew each of them would be comparing Callie to his ex-wife Stephanie which would not be fair given how different they were from the others. As Jason thought through the day's timing of events, Callie's visit at the cottage could not have happened that day.

"When did you see the girls?"

"Yesterday and this morning," Callie answered. "They let me sleep over in your bed. I hope you don't mind."

Callie smiled as she watched Jason visualize her in his bed.

"Missed you," she then added to both stir his juices and to reset expectations from last year that the rules had changed.

The waiter appeared as Callie took another sip of water to savor the sight of Jason in the candlelight. Having him there with her filled her with the joy she had been aching for long before their weekend reunion in the fall. Those two days of confessions, truth, and guidance from him became the tipping point that pushed her marital discord to divorce.

Jason ordered a glass of Cabernet to open the evening as Callie settled for a lighter French Rose'. Already half of a double bourbon into the evening, Jason knew he had to pace himself through dinner in order to navigate the dark country roads back to the farm. Callie took a large first taste of the Rose' as soon as it was placed in front of her. As she finished, Jason lifted his Cab and presented a toast for the evening.

"To the third act of life with the *ONE* perfect for you."

Callie loved the sentiment that he was directing toward her. She remembered his philosophy of a three-act life of youth, family, then empty-nest. She also remembered his comment that if you are lucky, the spouse you choose for family evolves with you to be right for the empty nest. She also recalled Rebecca clearly telling her before she left how it was obvious to her that Callie was Jason's *ONE*. The person he knew in his heart he was meant to be with. That same sentiment was reiterated by Jason to her before she headed back to Washington with her husband.

"To our third act," Callie repeated as she touched her glass to his.

Both took a drink excited about being together. But they wanted to be cautious about how things were to evolve from there. It was important to Jason, who had been thinking about this day for years, that things progress slowly. His goal was to create something lasting. Callie was emotionally drained and needed touched and held to tell her how vibrant and attractive she was. Going too fast could burn them too hot then out. Despite their obvious enthusiasm to be together, both Callie and Jason were fearful their renewed relationship had that potential.

# # # #

The sun that was hidden behind the mountains when they sat for dinner disappeared without notice. The candles that stood on each rail post as decoration earlier became the dining area's only source of light beyond the small table candles and the soft light that bled from the restaurant onto the deck. The evening moon that sat low on the horizon offered only a glistening streak of light over the water.

Their conversation that initially started as small talk diverted off into tangents that loosely touched on all aspects of Callie's life and children. As far as she could see, Jason's life was proceeding on a steady, unchanged course except for a twinge of suspicion about his feelings for Clara. But the fact that she knew him to be an honorable man, along with the way he acted at the beach last October despite being encouraged by Callie's short-term lapse in judgement, she knew Jason would not act upon any feelings for a married woman.

The most difficult part of the meal was when Callie admitted that the final straw for her that ended her marriage was Chase's repeated infidelities while on campaign assignments. It was a nagging suspicion she had for years that was finally verbalized to him for the first time at Jason's cottage in October. The irony that her accusation occurred at the time Chase caught Callie with Jason was not lost on any of them. Callie insisted on counseling to see if there was any hope to save their marriage. But when Chase returned to work and its extended travel after the New Year, those sessions got repeatedly put-off then ended along with her hopes for them as a couple.

"I know that was painful to go through and to talk about," Jason said as Callie looked sadly out over the water. "Steph and I talked about marriage counseling before we split. But there wasn't really anything to unearth. To me, it would have been paying someone to regurgitate all the things we already knew and were discussing."

Callie knew Jason was trying to console her through her process and failed counseling. But his situation was not theirs. Chase was hiding numerous affairs that were uncovered one-by-one through the sessions. Each admission shot an arrow into Callie's heart and soul. But as painful as each was, holding her family together was more important to her than the emotional scarring each affair created. She knew she could continue wounded if it benefitted her kids and kept her promise to God.

"Jason," she finally interjected. "Please, stop. I know you're trying to help. I really do. And I really appreciate it. But I'm getting past it on my own. This is just stirring it all back up."

"You'll have happiness in your life again," he answered to finish with something positive.

Callie's responded with a blank look to again ask for no more. The words he was saying made complete sense. But the emotional pain that still existed in her from both the betrayals and the failure of her to save her marriage was still raw and healing.

"I don't honestly know if I'll ever get over it," she answered. "I feel so cold inside right now."

"That too will go away," he said as he offered a reassuring smile. "Have faith that there is good to come in your life and your kid's life. That rat-bastard husband of yours will burn in hell and rot."

Callie smiled as she focused on her hands that were nervously wringing. As she looked to him, Jason offered a toast with his wine glass that Callie initially rejected with a look of exhaustion.

"Come on," he pleaded while holding his hand and glass over the candle. "Don't leave me hanging…. People are starting to look."

Jason's comment finished with an unexpected urgency. Callie's immediate feeling was one of embarrassment as she took hold of her glass while looking at the other tables for spectators. Not one person was either looking or quickly turned away as she surveyed the crowd. Knowing that she had been duped into accepting his toast, Callie's expression of panic changed to a smile of concession as she turned back to him. When she found his caring eyes still locked on her, his glass was still out in front of him hovering over the flame.

"Welcome to the North Carolina mountains," he said. "I can't tell you how delighted I am that you're here."

As Callie put her glass to his, the resulting sound of a slight clink introduced a soothing peace to her sadness. The day that started strangely then headed south through the drive, phone call, police stop, and pond surprise, was showing hope for recovery. As she looked at Jason, she noticed the same adoration in his eyes that he had in the fall. She now felt like she was where she needed to be. They ordered their desserts to go.

# # # #

When the valet pulled the Range Rover to the restaurant door, it did not stand out as anything special. The vehicles that were queued in the valet service included a Mercedes, Lexus and an older Porsche coupe with its Targa top removed. Callie's car continued to idle as Jason escorted her to her door that was opened for her. He slipped the valet ten dollars before getting in to drive home.

The two hours spent at Lakeside Inn was starting the process he hoped they would renew when he posted his innocuous Facebook post to find and lure her back to him. As Callie's phone paired to the Range Rover's Bluetooth system, a series of dings for missed texts and calls began filling the interior around them. Callie immediately changed the truck's display screen to keep everything private.

"I'm sorry," she said as she searched her clutch to disconnect her phone from the car. "I had it on silent because.... well, just because."

Callie did not want to finish her explanation. As she looked at her phone screen, calls from Lizzie, her mother Carolyn, and Chase were displayed as missed. Three unheard messages where shown on the voice mail icon. Four unread texts also listed.

"You're a popular person," Jason observed as she began thumbing through text messages.

"Just my kids and my mom wondering where I am," she answered keeping Chase's message to herself. "My daughter Lizzie called on my drive down here. She's lonely in Nantucket and wants to fly here to catch up with me."

"She's welcome to come," Jason replied honestly. "There's lots to do here. You can use the time to rebuild that relationship. It'd be good."

"But what about us? What about rebuilding our relationship?"

Jason took a moment to build a response. His pause worried Callie.

"We have the rest of our lives," he answered. "This is a delicate time I did alone with my kids. You may have to do that too because it's important to the rest of your life."

Callie's initial feeling to his words were appreciation that he was putting his wants and needs second to hers. It made sense that her working on any strain between her family would eliminate any hesitancy her kids would have to accept Jason as an important part of her life. Her confirmation for that was in how Jason's girls openly accepted her at the beach despite only having the advance knowledge and introduction to her through a mysterious photograph. And, not a good one at that.

"You would do that for me?" she asked almost afraid of the answer. "You'd let Lizzie come visit and stay in the cabin."

"Of course," he answered, without hesitating. "Drive my car, eat my food…. drink my wine."

Jason finished with a smile trying to break Callie out of her child-induced funk. Although the drinking age everywhere was twenty-one, Jason let his girls start experiencing alcohol first with wine at dinners, then beers on hot summer afternoons, and then a few years later, with Margaritas at the beach. True to Callie's forest-based child rearing observation that parents wear down as each child matures, Rachel's first wine was at sixteen, first beer at the beach was at eighteen, and first Margarita was somewhere around twenty. Jason could not date Maya's first wine. He did know her first Margarita, near him, was at seventeen.

"I don't know Jason. Seeing you with me may be more difficult for her than seeing her dad with…."

Callie stopped her comment not wanting to share what she knew about Lizzie's real reason to want to leave and Chase's bold shenanigans in Nantucket.

"With what?" Jason asked.

"It's not important," Callie replied. "I was always her buddy in Nantucket. So, she misses me."

"I get that. Well the offer still stands."

Jason sensed there was more to the story than what Callie was sharing. From his own divorce experience where his wife met her next *someone* soon after, he knew Callie's children, particularly her only daughter, would have difficulty with either of them finding someone new. Jason did not know if he was ever identified to her kids as part of their divorce discussions. If not during sessions, Jason suspected that Chase likely embellished and used that dirt privately with them to tarnish Callie's image.

Callie's eyes returned to her phone as she started to read a voice mail transcription from her mother. The words were choppy and mostly incorrect. Little of it made any sense beyond the fact that Carolyn had Facetimed with Lizzie. It amused her that her iPhone would transcribe the word *Facetime* when it botched much easier ones. Callie knew one of her texts was also from her mother. She shifted over to read it.

"My mom left me a message then sent me a text," she said as her screen opened.

Callie wanted to fill the dead air with a comment that would let her keep reading. The fact that they were now out of the town and off into the darkness of unlit country roads was lost to her. Jason smiled as he watched her do the same thing that irritated him about his kids.

"Tell her I said hello," he responded only to get a quick look of disbelief that returned to her screen.

"My mother is offering to fly Lizzie from Nantucket to Asheville to be with me. She thinks I'm alone and worried that I'm off by myself. She's asking if something happened AGAIN between you and me at the beach. She thinks mother-daughter time, as in me and Lizzie, would be good for both of us."

Callie dropped the phone into her lap as she looked out in the darkness.

"I'm surprised she didn't push that all three of us should tour the Biltmore together," she mumbled.

Jason cracked a smile then laughed as he watched Callie work through her frustration.

"She loves you," he said through a chuckle that told Callie he was joking.

"This isn't funny," she replied. "My life is so fucked up right now that... this isn't funny!"

Jason clenched his lips as he worked to retain a laugh to her first f-bomb. F-bombs were Callie's release to any anxiety that was building. It was her declarative adjective she used since she was a young child when life's frustrations grew to be too much. She told her parents that she learned the word from her older sister Patty when it inadvertently was hurled out when she was twelve. Callie broke into tears as they came to an intersection. Jason pulled the Range Rover onto the berm to console her.

"It's OK," he said. "It's going to be OK. You just have to work through it."

"Can we just go home?" she answered in frustration not realizing the word she had chosen. "I'll deal with this in the morning."

As the car merged back on to the road, Callie remained silent as she stared out the side window. She knew she would have to make a decision regarding Lizzie. Why Chase had called her still remained a mystery since she did not look to read the transcript of his voicemail. Her expectation was to suggest that she rid him of Lizzie so he could continue to play with his home-wrecking whore. To save Callie meant giving Chase more opportunity. The weight of the decision, and its ripple effects to her time with Jason, was proving painful.

# # # #

Jason returned to the cabin's living room area after changing back into cotton sleep pants and a Temple University t-shirt. Callie's bedroom door was closed to a crack with the light on behind it. Knowing she was struggling made him question how to finish their evening together. He expected her to stay in her room for the night. But he hoped, like in the fall, she would choose to find her way to him to just be held as she slept. The decisions all had to be hers. Her progression and comfort through it all were important for her, and for them.

Jason pulled the cork on a bottle of Cabernet and poured two healthy servings into the cabin's logo etched, stemless glasses. He dimmed the cabin lights to give Callie visibility through the room to the deck. He then grabbed the lighter to ignite the candles that were there for ambiance and bug control. The warm, humid air stood still as he turned from his last candle to the couch.

The initial excitement to find Callie curled on the couch was swamped by concern when she remained deep in thought. His presence and movement on the deck was unnoticed. As he walked toward her, her trance that was fixated out into the darkness did not break. He placed her wine on the table in front of her.

"Where did you think you would be at this stage in life?" she asked without moving.

"I don't remember ever thinking that far in advance," he answered. "But I'm sure I had visions of grandeur for the big house, the expensive car, and the trophy wife."

Jason studied Callie's face as he delivered the last item. It was intended to pull her back to him. Her reply was a look of disbelief.

"To the most desirable and *bestest* of them all," he smiled.

Callie stayed silent as she reached for her glass, took a drink, then watched as she swirled what remained in her glass.

"Don't get me wrong when you hear this, but I worked really hard to save my marriage.... I just thought you should know that."

Callie held her eyes on the swirl as Jason digested her words. He knew that when she left with Chase in the fall that his odds of seeing her again were next to none. Her level of commitment to keep her promises was almost a fatal flaw. He knew if she saw hope with Chase that their marriage would not break; and that he would have to move on. Her text to *wait for him* gave him hope that she would come back. Her complete silence until the pond swim had him ready to let go.

"I'm going to be honest too," Jason replied after thinking through Callie's confession. "I did not expect that I'd ever see you again. Then your text on Thanksgiving lit my world back up only to have it fade down to almost nothing again. It was hard to keep my promise not to call you after our weekend together. But I wasn't going to upset your cart to fill my own."

Callie moved to nestle in next to him as his arm reached around to secure her. Unlike their last time in October when the air was cool and blankets were needed to keep warm, the warm, humid, Blue Ridge mountain air around them became uncomfortable as their body heat came together. Jason could feel perspiration forming on his brow as Callie burrowed deeper into his hold. He ran his hand through his hairline to disburse the sweat while staying close to her.

"There was a voice message I didn't tell you about," Callie said from nowhere.

"I saw it on the car screen."

"He's only called me a few times over the past months mostly because of the Nantucket trip they're on now to coordinate the kids and to remind me that I wasn't invited to go."

"Would you have gone?"

"No, of course not," she answered immediately. "At least.... I don't think so."

Callie's change of direction concerned her. It was the first time she admitted that had she been given the opportunity that she may have gone despite the trip being with her unfaithful husband and his extended family. Jason watched as she rolled back through her comment and its implications.

"Do you want to go there?" he asked. "I'll fly you there and get your car back to your mom's."

Callie released a small laugh at the thought and offer.

"You buy a beach cottage when you really don't like the beach then move your entire life to the North Carolina shore just to position yourself two hours from my mother IN CASE my life and marriage is bad enough that I come find you.... AND IT WORKS!... Then you offer to send me back to him when your desired end-result happens... I just don't get you."

Callie's observation rattled Jason as he pulled together his response. It really did not make any sense from her point of view. He could tell her that she still had to finish her journey of separation to find the peace she needed to move one. That would be consistent with what he said she needed to do in the fall. But what he could not tell her was that, as the clocked ticked through the winter, spring and early summer, his expectation to see her again all but evaporated while his desire to find someone new started to bloom.

"I'm not that complicated of a person," he answered. "What we talked about in the fall is still true today. You have a shitload of things to work out before I come into the picture. Namely your daughter, your other kids, your MOM, and particularly that douche.... Douche? ... douche bag husband of yours."

Callie shared his humor through his reiterated description of Chase as a douche bag. It was a term she hated in any other context. But it was appropriate for how she felt about her husband now. As the humor of that subsided, a sadness followed to return her to a dark place.

"Yes," she agreed finally. "I thought I was well on my way. But the moment I take a few steps forward, new things get introduced to push me few steps back."

"As painful as that is. It's healthy. Trust me on that."

Jason squeezed Callie for support as the heat generated from their bodies was becoming too much to handle. He moved slowly to excuse himself using a bio call as his reason. As he stood, they both noted a large moist imprint of Callie on his shirt. Jason waved the fabric to unstick it from his body, to cool down, and to attempt to dry it. Callie smiled as she wiped her hand across her face noting her own perspiration.

"Never let them see you sweat," he said with a wink as he turned to head inside.

# # # #

As Jason disappeared into the cabin, Callie stood to stretch her legs. The sounds of the forest that came from the darkness were hypnotic. She pulled her phone from her pant pocket to check for more messages. The screen illuminated her face as it lit to show more texts from Lizzie and Carolyn.

Callie read through Carolyn's texts offering again to fly Lizzie to Asheville. The tone of her texts was getting stronger as Callie read the frustration her mother was having trying to reach her. The time displayed on her phone was after eleven. So, her expectation was that Carolyn was already in bed, and asleep, for the night. Callie knew the same would not be true for her daughter.

"I'm sorry to have been quiet today," she texted. "I'll talk to you in the morning."

As Callie pushed send the dots appeared below her text that indicated that Lizzie was already crafting her reply.

"Gram said she would pay for my flight. Dad said he didn't care."

Pressure began building inside Callie to surrender to let Lizzie come. But having her there would infringe on the personal time she needed with Jason to reestablish their relationship.

"I know. I am getting texts from ALL of you," Callie texted back. "let's talk tomorrow."

Jason was standing in the doorway waiting for Callie to finish her texting. He knew it was to either Lizzie or Carolyn. He also knew Carolyn was likely in bed by now. As Callie dropped her phone down from her face and its light went dark, Jason slid the screen door open.

"That's good timing," Callie said as she looked at the bottle he was carrying.

"I waited until you were finished," he confessed. "Lizzie?"

Callie smiled at the question knowing he had four times the experience with girls. He knew not only would Lizzie be up, but that she would be on her phone.

"Yes," Callie answered. "I'm getting battered with pressure to let her come here. And, I can't."

Jason poured the last drops of wine into her glass that was sitting on the table. He watched her struggle with her decision as he handed some grape-based sedative to her.

"Then don't," he stated which was contrary to everything he had said before.

To invite Lizzie to Jason's cabin and to have to explain Jason to her was frightening. For all of Chase's misgivings and bad deeds, he never used Callie's Columbus Day weekend with Jason last October to harm her in front of her children. He was brutal with it in discussions with the lawyers. But he never, to her knowledge, used it to tarnish her with her children.

"This is too much to explain," she replied. "I'd have to get my own cabin."

Jason's expression sank with that declaration. He agreed that it was likely the best thing to introduce Lizzie to him and his world. But he also knew all the cabins were all taken.

"You've got to be fucking kidding me," Callie exclaimed when he told her.

"Callie, it's July, not February. It's high season."

Callie grew frustrated as her solution evaporated.

"Then you should cozy up with little miss property manager and work a deal. She's using your car. How about a little quid-pro-quo for a place to stay?"

Jason did not find humor in the suggestion.

"It's just not possible," he answered.

"Then what?"

Jason had a thought he knew Callie would not like. He could stay in the main house with Clara. The manager's quarters had two bedrooms.

"You make your plans," he said. "Let me see what I can do in the morning."

As they finished their wine, Callie snuggled back next to Jason for support. But when the heat made things uncomfortable again, both stood to find air and to cool. Jason watched Callie work through a progression of her shirt and pants to ensure all the wrinkles were pulled straight. When she finally finished, she looked up to see him smiling back at her.

"What?"

"Just stand there," he answered. "The glow of the candle on your tanned face and hair is stunning."

Callie damned the heat and sweat for what she needed to do. As he stood in silence appreciating every inch of her being, she sauntered to him to press her body to his and to kiss his smile away. The taste of the wine on his lips permeated to hers as she kissed him again. And the heat they sought to escape through separation grew hotter.

# # # #

Callie held Jason's hand as they walked back through the living room. Their pace was casual giving each time to think through what the next step should be for their first night together in the Blue Ridge Mountains. As they approached the front hall, the doors to each bedroom sat on opposite sides of the hallway. Jason stopped first then turned to Callie. For the first time, she stood there nervous in front of him with the freedom to act on any wish she had as if it was their first time together. His face showed the same adoration she remembered from both October as well as when they dated and became engaged to be married. There was no doubt in Callie's heart to whether the man looking at her loved her.

"I think we should sleep in different rooms tonight," he said to her surprise. "Like I said in the fall, I want you to be sure. And… I don't think you are."

Callie's heart broke with the statement. Their history and her availability had all evolved to make this moment perfect.

"I don't understand," she replied. "Is something wrong?"

Jason smirked at the comment.

"No," he answered. "It's too right. So, I want you to be sure."

"Is it the owner's wife?" Callie asked as her thoughts became unchecked words.

Jason stepped back to look at her. He knew there was some truth to it. But Callie's verbalization rattled him.

"What would make you ask that question?"

"I don't know. I watched you two play in the pond. I have a husband who had women other than me on the side. I just don't trust anything now. So, I have these suspicions."

Callie's eyes teared with her desperate confession. She had just insinuated that Jason was cheating on her or, at least, holding back a competitive love interest.

"Just relax," he answered. "Let life play itself out for you to enjoy."

Jason pulled Callie close to give her the comfort and support she needed and a soft kiss for reasssurance. As she separated to her room, he put the two dogs out the front door and waited. When they returned, Molly nosed into Callie's room as he and Zoe walked outside to extinguish the candles on the deck. Jason knew that tomorrow was going to be difficult as Callie worked through her details with Lizzie; and, he made arrangements to make to make it all work.

As he flipped the last switch to the living room lights, a night light automatically lit in the front hall. Zoe had romped ahead and was already curled at the foot of his bed in the light brown mark that designated her spot in the comforter. Jason finished with a run through the bathroom and retired to his bed to find her asleep.

As he discovered at the beach when Callie visited, sleeping was not going to be easy. As time ticked by on the digital clock that sat on his nightstand, Jason laid still wondering if taking the honorable route again this time with sleeping arrangements, and possible sex, was the right thing to do. He had a overpowering hesitation building within him that was telling him to wait. As a young man, it would have been easy to ignore that inner voice for the simple pleasures of being with a willing partner in the moment. But at fifty-six years of age, his perspective was different and partially driven by his lower performing libido combined with his natural fear of failure on the first attempt with someone new. Jason exhaled as he found comfort in putting off that moment of truth for at least one more night.

The silence in the house was the same as it was when he was alone with Zoe. Her periodic snoring annoyed him sometimes making it necessary to give her a firm, but polite, push off the bed to go find other accommodations. But tonight, Zoe was quietly sleeping as whispers of air could be heard from her breathing. Jason felt his anxiety release and was ready to sleep.

"I'm sorry," Callie apologized as she forged into his room wrapped in her blanket. "I won't sleep unless I'm here. I'm sorry."

Her determination as the door flew open making her appear in ghost-like fashion amused and aroused him. He rolled a complete turn to open the nearside of the bed for her. Zoe woke to the commotion and was already out the door looking for a new place to nest. Both Callie and Jason had the same expectation as she laid down next to him, still wrapped in the blanket, and facing the wall. As she settled, she reached back pull him close. Jason slid his body to hers and spooned to her shape. Both then took one final breath and drifted off to sleep together.

10

The sun streak that was created by a gap in the window at Jason's cottage at the beach in the morning to wake Callie did not appear in the cabin. The trees that were overtop the cabin created a canopy where light filtered in loosely. The shades in the room were not room darkening and did not need to be. They were only to obstruct sight lines in from the outside.

The glow of the morning light started just after 6AM and consistently grew brighter. Jason always woke refreshed to the natural sunlight. Translucent window shades would have been something he knew his ex-wife would have swapped out just after the purchase. At least in the rooms where she slept.

Callie woke refreshed having experienced her best night's sleep in months. She remembered the same effect while she was at the beach. Her sleep there was heavy and refreshing too.

As Callie's bladder began to wake with her, she moved to make a quick visit to the bathroom before starting her first day with Jason over a cup of coffee on the deck. Her excitement, however, diminished as she thought through her list for the day that included telling Lizzie she could not visit. She would have to create an excuse. Lizzie likely still believed her Asheville trip was solo.

Callie continued to run options as she tried to release herself from the blanket she brought to his room. She smiled remembering the first morning last fall when she woke to find Zoe snuggled beside her after Jason went for his swim. Since there was no ocean and no swimmable lake nearby, Callie began to slowly work her way free from the bind of the blanket to seek her refuge on the toilet. After a final slight tug that resulted in a grumble from behind, she knew she was free. And, as she looked back satisfied to have not woken him through her effort, Zoe again wagged her tail in appreciation that Callie did not shove her off the bed. A sense of Déjà vu set in as Callie again left Zoe in Jason's bed to go find him after their first night together.

As in the fall when she appeared in his living room, Callie noticed the smell of coffee and that Jason was nowhere to be found. A set of Fox Farm mugs sat to the right of the coffee maker which made her smile in remembrance of the strategically placed *raddest dad* mug he left for her before heading out for his early morning swim. As she filled her cup, she continued to look and to listen around the small rustic setting for him. Like his daughters at the beach, he was probably going to be found on the deck in the warm air instead of in the air conditioning they enjoyed overnight. Before she moved to find him, Molly and Zoe appeared from her bedroom looking for breakfast.

Callie gave each dog a quick bowl of food pulling from Jason's supply. Her serving to Zoe was a guess based on how much she served Molly. Both dogs quickly took to their bowls as if racing the other to see who could finish first. When they finished, each went to investigate the other's bowl for what was left. Both dogs were disappointed.

As the two dogs enjoyed their breakfast, Callie strolled to the closed sliding door to check the deck for Jason. Everything was in place as she remembered it. And, like at the beach in October, he was not found on it.

It seemed strange to Callie that Jason was gone. There was no note left to indicate where he went or if he was going to return at any given time. The clock in the kitchen read 9:30 AM which was an unusual sleep-in for her. Her habit was to usually rise before 8 AM. It was much earlier when her kids where at home.

As she sat on the living room sofa finding herself alone again, the front door swung open as the crinkling of a bag made its way through the cabin.

"I forgot to order breakfast," Jason said as he placed the bag on the counter. "Fortunately, Clara had extras she could share. I hope you don't mind a junkier food breakfast?"

Callie stood and sauntered over to the counter to check Jason's find. She recalled the pastries at the beach and always appreciated a good one from time to time. These, however, were more to the tune of muffins. But she was hungry and not going to be either picky or rude to point that out.

"This is perfect," she said. "We can go shopping today to get some food for the week."

Jason stayed quiet as he pondered her comment. While visiting the main house and having his first awkward conversation with Clara, he confirmed what he already knew. The *Flying Dutchman* was committed for the rest of the summer starting in two days. The cabin Callie was now calling home was going to service other people for the foreseeable future.

"There may be a slight problem with that," he said. "This cottage is committed for the summer in two days."

"Oh my God," Callie chuckled. "I completely lost myself in this place. Are there any others?"

"No," Jason answered. "I checked while I was at the main house."

Callie pondered the situation as she unpacked the muffins. The unavailability of the cabin meant that she had an excuse for Lizzie not to visit. Her comfort was short-lived when she realized that Lizzie would suggest finding somewhere else to stay. She looked to Jason for help.

"Let's just have coffee and breakfast on the deck. I have some errands to run that you can help me with. It'll show you more of what's around here."

Callie picked up the plate of muffins and her cup of coffee.

"Did you by chance make me one?" Jason asked remembering the same situation from the fall.

"No Jason," she exhausted. "I didn't. Is that my job?"

Callie knew his question was a rehash of that fun moment. She used the same reply to keep it going. Jason responded with an appreciative smile as he reached for a Fox Farm mug to fill with his own blend of coffee, sweat-n-low and half-n-half. He followed Callie to the door and opened it to the heat for her first full day back with him.

# # # #

Callie intended to stay the two final days in the cabin with Jason. It was quiet and nestled in the trees for privacy. She was also growing to like the simple but elegant amenities it offered. But to make the next two days work, she knew they would have to stop at a grocery to get items for snacks and meals to keep their time intimate before heading back to a house filled with his daughters and their friends.

Jason took the plate back into the house as he excused himself for a bathroom break. As he was returning to the deck, he heard the clanging of church bells bellow through the door as Callie picked up her phone. Knowing from the fall that church bells were her mother's dedicated ring tone, Jason stopped to watch what happened instead of returning through the door back into the confusion.

"Hi mom," Callie answered.

Carolyn was seated on a stool overlooking her kitchen island. She had her laptop open to flight apps to see what it would take to fly Lizzie to Callie with the least amount of transfers and at the best price.

"Callie, where are you?" Carolyn exclaimed. "Lizzie said you're in the mountains and not at the beach. Did something go wrong with Jason? I knew that was a bad idea."

Callie was waiting for the declaration of foresight that always came from her mother when she could declare being right after the fact. Callie did a quick look for Jason who was nowhere to be seen. It was comfortable to speak honestly.

"He wasn't at the beach. He's here in Asheville... or at least on some farm of cabins near Asheville. I don't know what this is about. It's certainly not my choice for a vacation."

"Well, that certainly changes things," Carolyn declared. "I was ready to buy Lizzie a plane ticket to get her to you for moral support."

"Moral support?" Callie laughed. "Mom, I'm in a cabin in the mountains with a man she doesn't know even exists, let alone my history with him."

"Well, I didn't know that sweetie. I'm just trying to do what's best for both of you."

"Jason just told me we're heading back to the beach the day after tomorrow."

"Are you sleeping with him Callie? You know you're still married in God's eyes. I'm not comfortable with..."

"Mom!" Callie cut her off in a harsh whisper. "Chase screwed multiple women when he was married to me. I think God will forgive me if I jump the gun here. I mean. If I choose for that to happen."

Callie felt uncomfortable talking about her sexual activity with her mother. Despite it being entirely natural and encouraged by the church to create the next generations of devout followers and donors, talk of sex with her mother was particularly painful from the day the topic first presented as a teenager.

"Callie!"

"Mom, please. Just mind your own business for once!" Callie answered in a voice was direct and hurtful.

"But..."

Callie's patience with her mother's judgement on her sex life with anyone but Chase had just run out. She was angry at her and at the situation. She pushed the button on her phone to abruptly end the debate. Hanging up on her mother was a rare occurrence and always had notable kick-back the next time they were together.

As Carolyn put her phone down on the counter, she closed her eyes to soothe the rejection she just received. She then closed her laptop to get on with her day deleting all of the research she had done to get Lizzie to Callie.

# # # #

Callie remained still while internally debating whether she should call her mother back and apologize. The changes in her life had ripple effects that affected her mother's sense of family and deep religious faith. Out of wedlock sex was another taboo item that her mother would not tolerate. However, that issue had already been debated when Callie admitted having been with Jason while they dated.

"I need to run out to get the Jeep from the repair shop," Jason said after sliding the glass door open. "Do you want to come?"

Callie heard only a part of his invitation as it pulled her out of deep thought.

"Go where?" she asked.

"To get the Farm's Jeep at the shop," Jason repeated. "You OK?"

Jason sat next to Callie on the sofa. She was laid out in a mermaid position with her feet extending toward him. As he sat, she curled up to give him a seat on the end cushion.

"I'm just peachy," she smiled with a notable look of anxiety. "I just hung up on my mother. She wanted to know if we had sex last night. I told her *yes*."

The declared answer to the question lit Callie's face as Jason sat stunned. Although he and Callie were both in their fifties with children, the thought of her mother thinking they had sex bothered him.

"Why..."

"I told her to mind her own business," Callie interrupted to ease his disbelief. "I didn't say we had sex. So, don't get all stressed out."

"That's better," he agreed now stroking her leg. "Although...."

Jason's devilish look conveyed the message he wanted to send. Callie smiled already thinking ahead to the uncomfortable call she had to make to Lizzie. As she took his hand that was rubbing her calf, she smiled a reassuring look.

"I've got to call Lizzie to cancel," she said. "Why don't you go get the Jeep. We can go out for the day after you get back; and I'm cleaned up."

Jason patted Callie's bum as he went to stand. Although rejected for the moment, there was still hope for the afternoon or evening. He gave a quick wave with his smile loaded with disappointment as he headed back into the cabin.

Callie waited for the door to slide shut before picking up her phone. As it lit, she looked at the picture on the home screen of her kids with her mother in Williamsburg. The picture was taken on Easter Sunday during the last time her oldest son, Michael, was home. The previous picture of the family, that included Chase, was removed and deleted. Seeing her mother's eyes looking back at her from her screen made her feel guilty for having been so rude.

"Hello," grumbled a groggy girl voice.

"Lizzie, it's mom."

"I know mom," she answered. "Your picture appears on my screen when you call."

"I'm sorry to be calling so early," Callie lied with a smile, "I need to talk to you about Asheville and your grandmother."

The two references sat Lizzie upright with excitement. Her grandmother had convinced her mom that she should leave Nantucket for a better time in North Carolina.

"So, I'm coming?" she asked. "When's my flight?"

"No sweetie, I can't make that happen."

"Why!? Gram said she'd pay for it… I've flown before…"

Lizzie had her argument points pre-packaged to throw at her mother. It was a genetic gift from her dad who could rattle out bullet points to any argument at any time.

"I'm leaving here tomorrow," Callie interrupted.

"Oh, are you going home?" Lizzie inquired. "I'll come home. That's even cheaper."

As she spoke, Lizzie flipped her Instagram open to see if her friends were at home and posting. Being early in the morning, nothing new appeared from the night before. Therefore, she knew at least some were still at home.

"I'm not going home," Callie struggled to say.

"I guess I could fly to Richmond and you could get me from Grams," Lizzie responded now dejected about her prospect of going somewhere fun.

"Your Gram would really love to see you. But I'm not going there either."

"Geez, mom. This is like Where's Waldo. Then where are you going?" Lizzie asked then gasped to excitement. "Are you going to the beach to visit that friend from last fall? Stephanie? I think."

"Yes," Callie cringed. "I'm going there for a week or so."

"Can I go there with you!? You did say *next time* when we talked last fall"

Callie exhaled to being held to a promise she made when trying to get out a dicey conversation of where she was last fall. *Fuck*, she mouthed into the air.

"Sweetie, it's a small cottage and their kids will be there. They'll likely put kids on the couches to give me a room."

"So, I'll sleep with you," Lizzie interjected.

Callie smiled as her immediate thought was that Lizzie was not the person she wanted to sleep with at the beach.

"Honey, I can't do that last minute. Next time. I promise."

"Well that sucks," Lizzie said deflated to the loss of all the options she had. "You could've waited until later to tell me all of that."

Callie empathized with her daughter's disappointment while enjoying a slight joy of having rousted her from sleep on vacation.

"I'll see you in a week or so," she replied. "Be good. Enjoy the beach."

As Callie finished, she watched her screen switch from Lizzie back to the phone's home screen. Lizzie was gone before Callie could finish her goodbye.

11

Jason honked as he pulled down to the main house kitchen door. He could see Clara in the window that sat over the kitchen sink. As Clara looked up to see, Jason waved from inside the car and motioned for her to come out.

"Look at you in your pimped-out, drug lord ride," she joked as she sauntered down slowly from the porch.

Seeing him in Callie's car created mixed emotions. The first was that he was driving her extraordinarily expensive car without her which set a level of trust between them. The second was that Callie was not with him. He was riding solo giving her some time to be with him.

"Jerry has the Jeep ready," Jason stated as Clara rested her hands on the door. "Can you ride with me to get it?"

The ride to Jerry's Auto Shop was a ten-minute roundtrip. Clara looked around the main house for activity. No one was walking about; and, she expected no incoming food for brunch.

"Sure," she answered. "Let me put the sign on the front desk.

Clara disappeared back into the main house as Jason sat waiting. A smile erupted on her face as she entered the kitchen. She visited the small powder room located off the main hall for a status check. Her hair looked good and wispy. She quickly did a few smacks on her cheeks to liven their color then straightened her Fox Farm shirt before heading back out.

"Sign in place?" Jason asked.

"What?" she responded with a puzzled look. "YES! The sign. Yes.

It's in its place."

Clara quickly looked away with an expression of relief as she felt for the seatbelt.

As they left the property, Jason stepped on the accelerator to quickly pass the posted speed limit on Blackburn Road. Clara felt herself sink into her seat as she watched the speedometer quickly reach sixty miles per hour and keep climbing. It was the same amount of time the farm's Jeep would take to reach forty.

"Fancy ride," she said as she lightly moved her hand across the leather arm rest.

"Expensive ride," Jason added.

"Expensive buys fancy."

Jason smiled to the comment as he unconsciously put his hand on Clara's arm to show his amusement. The sensation from his touch stopped her breathing. As he let go, Clara looked out her window to exhale softly and silently. The next few minutes were silent which Clara used to admire Jason as she pretended to relish the car's interior.

"Here we are," Jason said as they pulled into Jerry's.

Clara studied the familiar, old gas station and its seventy-five-year-old owner who was standing out front in his oil-soaked coveralls. Jason slowly pulled the Range Rover to him before lowering his tinted window.

"Jerry!" he said as he rolled down his window.

"Damn son, I thought you was one of those damn Yankees when you pulled in."

"I am," Jason replied matter-of-factly with a smile. "But I'm southern educated."

Jason's southern Virginia liberal arts education at Hampden-Sydney College in Virginia was his saving grace with Jerry and most of the older, established residents in the area. Although a lot of Yankees had been pouring into the region for decades, locals still welcomed them with the expected snarky Yankee jabs just for sport. Jerry gave an appreciative nod to the comment as Jason and Clara stepped out.

"We still have to decide whether Virginia is southern," Jerry joked as he patted Jason on the back.

Clara found the banter between Jason and Jerry charming as she immediately looked for an oil mark on Jason's shirt after Jerry pulled his hand away.

As Jason opened and held the door to the station's office, the two gentlemen waited for Clara to walk in first. As Jerry nodded for Jason to go before him, he smiled and winked a nod toward Clara whose back was too them. An immediate smile and look of agreement filled Jason's face as he walked in ahead of the old man. Jerry laughed as he gave Jason a second pat on the back.

The feel of Jerry's office dated back to a long, lost automotive era. Its floor had a patina of oil and dirt that made it feel gritty and slippery at the same time. The air was thick with a smell of tire rubber and grease. As Clara looked at the automotive artifacts adorning the walls, she wondered if the smell was going to stick to her clothing and hair.

Jason handed Jerry his Fox Farm Mastercard for payment after he was presented the repair bill. After Jason signed the charge slip, the three engaged in conversation about the room decorations. Jerry stapled the signed charge slip to the repair bill as he told a story about a glass clock that hosted an old, local oil company logo. When he finished with a chuckle, he handed Jason the paperwork and Jeep keys.

"Which car do you want to drive back," Jason asked with a grin as he held the Jeep keys in one hand and the Range Rover key fob in the other.

"Seriously?"

"Why not?"

Without hesitation, Clara reached for the Range Rover key

fob. As the exchange happened, Jason held onto her hand and grinned. The sensation stopped her breathing again.

"No funny business."

"There is the creek to the back property," Clara said with an aloof sarcasm as she turned and opened the door to leave the building. She then looked back with a devilish grin. Jerry, who was showing a smile in desperate need of a couple implants, laughed as he looked to Jason who was now beginning to regret his offer.

"You go girl," he added excited to be compounding Jason's stress.

The two men walked outside the office door to watch Clara pull out and accelerate away heavily on Blackburn Road. Jerry put his hand on Jason's shoulder again as they listened to the roar of the engine as it ran through the gears. Jason smiled feeling good that he gave Clara some fun, even if only for a few minutes back to the farm. As he looked to say good-bye to Jerry, the old man's facial expression said what Jason was thinking.

"She's a filly, that one," he stated. "If I were a young man…"

Jerry finished his thought with a heavy laugh and a final pat on Jason's back before pointing him to the farm's celery green, 1991 Jeep Grand Wagoneer parked near the garage bay.

# # # #

As he drove through the gates at Fox Farm, Jason checked to ensure the Range Rover had made it back safely. Jerry's work on the farm's Grand Wagoneer solved the pulling Jason felt when he drove to Asheville to meet with his attorneys. For fun, he decided to take the Jeep up to the *Flying Dutchman* to show Callie.

Jason knew from both history and their fall conversations that Callie was not a car girl. She was not going to appreciate any classic vehicle of any make unless it was a sports car. This Grand Wagoneer, however, was different. In its day, the Grand Wagoneer was the American version of her Range Rover. Rugged on the outside, yet nicely appointed on its inside. Callie's mother drove the same vehicle back when he and Callie dated and were engaged. It was the car he drove to Washington, D.C. to move her back to Pittsburgh for their wedding that was cancelled five weeks prior to its date. Jason found the Jeep on an auction website and thought its elegance fit the nature of Fox Farm. The Wagoneer was in Raleigh, spotless, and in excellent mechanical condition. After a quick visit to inspect it, Jason bought the vehicle on the spot.

The Jeep's padded leather seats and suspension system made the roads to the cabin as smooth as highway. As he reached the top of the hill that dropped down to the Flying Dutchman, Jason sounded the horn to announce he had arrived.

Callie exited the cabin excited to get their day moving. As she turned from closing the door, she froze in recollection to the sight of the car.

"This is crazy," she said. "I thought the farm Jeep was a Jeep… Jeep, not my mom's old car."

"Hop in," Jason replied. "Let's go run some errands before Clara realizes I didn't bring it back."

Callie enthusiastically opened the door then climbed up onto the plush passenger seat. As she looked around, she was impressed by its brand-new look. She ran her hand across the center armrest she remembered. She then spun to look to the back seat and storage area that had the carpeting her mother's Wagoneer had.

"This is like Déjà vu," she exclaimed. "Let's go to the view you showed me yesterday."

The suggestion surprised Jason. He knew Callie was nervous when they drove the fire road up to the site. But, her excitement to be reliving her mom's old car was bringing back some memories she had driving that Grand Wagoneer over some hills and streams in Western Pennsylvania.

"I'm not taking this car on that road," Jason announced.

Callie stopped her survey of the Jeep to look at him.

"You took my car up there?"

Jason was amused by her objection and held a laugh as he looked to the side mirror for no reason. After composing himself, he turned back to Callie to explain why.

"Callie, this car is a classic," he explained with a tint of sarcasm. "Your car, is a BEAST."

The difference made no sense to Callie. Both were big, powerful machines. Her SUV cost over one hundred thousand dollars. The Wagoneer they were riding in cost far less even when it was new. Callie interpreted his answer as her car being disposable while his was a treasure.

As she shifted her body to face forward again, Jason turned onto to the main driveway toward the front gate and Blackburn Road. Callie noticed Jerry's Auto's receipt that had fallen to the floor and picked it up. She admired the old format of the work order, the design of his logo, and the handwritten details and math. As she looked at the payment receipt, she was surprised by the low cost of the work. She then became fixated on the signature that signed the Fox Farm charge receipt.

"Why did you sign the charge receipt?"

Jason gave a look of confusion then looked at the paper. The charge receipt Jerry had stapled to the work order was the one he was supposed to keep.

"Oh, that old coot," Jason replied. "He stapled the wrong receipt copy to the work paper. We can stop on our way to give it back."

Callie continued to watch Jason as he looked away from the paper to put his eyes back on the road.

"Jason? Why are you paying for Clara's car repair?"

Callie tone was showed her irritation that he did not answer her question. As she looked again at his signature, she noted the charge name of the credit card holder as *Jason Cartwright, Fox Farm*.

"SURPRISE!" Jason declared with a forced expression and his hands up in the air.

"You work there?" Callie asked.

Jason let her thoughts catch up to her question. As the answer became clear, she looked back at the work order.

"You bought that place?" she verbalized in monotone and disbelief.

Callie's stomach pitted as Jason nodded his answer. In the nine months she took to free herself for him, he had made a big business investment in the mountains where she loved to visit but did not want to live for any length of time. As she exhaled her anguish, she looked out through the windshield to the endless passing of forest. To stay with Jason would likely make this her new home. *Fuck*, she thought to herself.

"It's exciting, isn't it?" Jason said anxious to break the silence.

As they pulled back into Jerry's to exchange charge receipts, Callie looked away thinking *exciting* was not the first word that came to mind. When she tuned back into her current surroundings, she looked at the old dilapidated gas station with disdain. Its elderly owner, who was missing a few teeth, began to scare her. Jason's new life was not what she expected. Her thoughts then rolled to Clara and how she, and her husband, assuming he was even still around, fit into this new picture. The mountains began to worry her.

"God help me," she whispered.

# # # #

The grocery store was old and quaint just like one would have been in Mayberry. The wooden shelves had neatly lined rows of items. Callie's first impression was appreciation for the history and subtle elegance of the building and business. But as she started looking for the specific items she wanted that they did not have, her appreciation of the Whole Foods back in Northern Virginia made this store a lot less appealing.

Jason greeted the counter clerk like they were old friends. His casual way blended into the country living he appeared to be adopting. It was apparent that his ability to work a conversation to win a friend was how he succeeded in business, won acceptance with the Abbies at the beach, and was winning over the folks around Fox Farm.

Callie drifted back to the meats section that hosted an impressive assortment of protein. As she studied the different cuts, the price per pound displayed surprised her. The meat was impressive. The prices compared to her D.C. area Whole Foods were unbelievable. Callie ordered two Rib Eye steaks while getting some asparagus and small potatoes to build dinner. While fish would have been the natural selection for their first grilled meal at the beach, steak was more appropriate for her mountain man.

"Did you find everything you wanted?" Jason asked as she approached with her basket.

"I did," Callie answered as she smiled at him then to the clerk.

"Fantastic," he answered. "I'll also take a mason bottle of Uncle Chub's."

The clerk nodded as he reached under the counter to produce the mason jar of brown liquid that had no label. Jason pulled cash from his wallet to pay for the groceries and the other mountain product that scared Callie.

"You'll like this," he whispered to her as they started to the door.

Callie looked at him with disbelief wondering who her man had become; and, what did she miss during their fall weekend that should have given her insight into the possibility for all of this unfolding?

As the Wagoneer started, Callie was reminded of the things she had uncovered. She looked at Jason as he backed the car from the front porch of the country store. His presence was what she remembered. His choices and new behavior were what she was finding troubling.

"Who are you? And, where is Jason Cartwright?" she asked with serious intent but in a joking manner.

Jason's surprise to the question caused him to pause to answer.

"What do you mean?"

"Who are you?" she repeated. "Where's that sophisticated guy I saw last fall with all the strategies to make things happen, to win friends, who, who, who...."

"Drove a piece of shit Wrangler and lived in a dumpy little beach cottage?" he jokingly finished for her.

"Yeah, that guy!" Callie agreed with a frustrated look.

"I'm right here."

"But what have you done in the last nine months? You've changed your life... again!"

"What's wrong?"

"I don't know.... Everything? Maybe?"

Jason saw Callie struggling as she tried to question him without offending him. A warmth of compassion filled him as he began to realize that she was not as excited about this new venture as he was. And, maybe it was because he made the decision and investment without consulting her. The problem he faced, however, was that they were not communicating at the time it all had to happen.

"You don't like it here," he said as a statement instead of a question.

Callie knew she did not have an option that would convey her true feelings without either upsetting or disappointing him. She thought of her house in Virginia with its manicured lawn and great views onto other like properties. Switching from that to a mountain life even near so many very cool areas was not an attractive change for her. Callie knew she was a city girl. Her expectation was that even though Jason was living in a beach cottage when they reconnected, he was thinking beyond that existence to build opportunities either in or near a big city. The beach also had the added appeal of being a two-hour drive to her mother. For the short term, the beach was a good life option to be near her while also with him.

"It's not like or dislike," she finally answered. "This is just all at once and so different to what I expected…. and am used to."

Callie felt good that she skirted the issue while still addressing his question. That talent was something her husband would appreciate with an *atta-girl*. Jason appeared to accept her explanation as he put the car into drive and pulled back onto the state road back to Fox Farm.

"Just give the dust a chance to settle," Jason said showing empathy for the shock she was feeling. "It certainly gets rid of the salt, sun and sand issues I have with the beach."

His humor fell flat as Callie just stared off into the distance.

"I like the salt, sun and sand of the beach," she replied in a sad, slow cadence.

"I do too," Jason agreed as he reached for her arm to comfort her. "And, we'll have that too. Clara is the on-site management of the property. I'm just the owner whose brought in for the big things and enjoys doing some work when needed. I will need to be here from time to time, and sometimes for extended periods. But I miss my friends at the beach. And, I do appreciate, AND

MISS, times in the city too. Just hang in there."

Callie smiled as she listened to Jason clear a lot of doubt from her head. She and Chase had friends that owned businesses throughout Virginia and beyond. So, having investments far away from where he lived started to become more palatable to her. He was still open to live near a decent city while holding on to her love at the beach and his near Asheville.

As they pulled into Fox Farm, Jason drove back to the Cabin to drop Callie and the groceries off. As she stepped out of the Wagoneer, she again studied the cabin and property that surrounded it. The rustic wood structure lit by the filtered sunlight that flowed through the leaves above it seemed bigger and better than her first impression. Callie waved to Jason as he pulled away to return the Jeep and to get her car from Clara.

12

Clara saw the Jeep return to the property then turn to go back up the drive to the *Flying Dutchmen*. That was the one benefit she liked about living at the main house. Otherwise, it felt like a fishbowl for everyone to watch.

Clara knew Jason had a fondness for the farm's Grand Wagoneer that she did not share. If she had a choice, Fox Farm would be represented by the black Range Rover that was currently parked by the kitchen door. The Wagoneer, however, did have a certain panache she enjoyed when driving it through town. It was also a significant step up from the Subaru Outback she and Tom had as their first company vehicle.

Jason parked the Wagoneer behind the Range Rover. As he walked toward the Main house, he looked back at the two machines admiring their distinctly different grace and beauty.

"They're cars, not works of art," Clara joked in a snarky tone to embarrass him.

"Look at those two beasts," he answered. "Both define the elegance of their time. What was perfect back in the 1990's when I was young is woefully dated and only appreciated by a few today."

"Well, if you're asking for my opinion," Clara said pausing to be sure she had his attention, "I vote for the Range Rover."

Clara's face showed she was anticipating a quick snarky comeback that Jason could not produce. He shook his head slightly as he reached to hand her the Wagoneer keys. As their hands touched, a warmth radiated again that made Clara pull back and blush slightly.

"I have the Range..." she stuttered. "I have your keys on the counter inside."

Clara caught her foot on the grassy incline as she turned back toward the main house. Her stumble felt more awkward than it looked. Jason instinctively reached to grab what he could to keep her from falling. But the quickness of her stumble put her out of his reach. After a few, quick, stuttered steps, Clara kept upright and continued on without looking back at him.

As she disappeared from view, Clara took a moment to stop and breath. The blush that she felt had to be obvious to him. Her stumble had to look ridiculous. The only thing that may have saved her was not expelling a giddy, girlish laugh of embarrassment after recovering from her stumble. Clara shook her head as she began to look for Clara's keys.

The key fob to the Range Rover that she thought was on the counter was not there. Clara started to panic as she looked nervously on the other tables and on the floor.

"Thought I'd come in for a drink," Jason said as he appeared in the doorway.

As he scanned the kitchen for Clara, he heard a stir as she reappeared from searching under the table.

"I can't find them," she laughed.

Jason's eyes bulged to the surprise. *That's not good* was his initial thought. He helped with a quick survey of the room only to find his car keys on the peg board by the back door.

"Well, I'll just take my car down," Jason said. "I'm sure they'll turn up. Besides, the two regal beasts add some cachet to the place. I kind of like it. Just let me know when you find them. We'll come back to get her car. Unless you want to drive it down by way of, say, Asheville?"

Jason smiled as Clara eyes darted upward to show agreement.

The thought had not crossed her mind until then.

"They're here. I will find them," she answered. "I'll bring it down to you."

# # # #

Jason walked across the grass to the pole building that hosted the work shed and covered parking for the property vehicle and tractor. He smiled as he recalled Clara's stumble up the grass hill and then her quick stand as she entered the kitchen. Her panicked look and tussled hair were beautiful. It was obvious that the dark sadness of losing her husband was finally leaving her.

As he approached the barn, Jason pushed the key fob to unlock his car. The 2015 steel blue Volvo Cross-Country station wagon was his favorite car to date. It replaced an older Acura MDX SUV that was more like the Range Rover Callie was driving without either the pedigree or the price tag. The Volvo was all wheel drive and a nice change from the bigger Acura. It was faster from a dead stop and had a generous cargo area to carry Zoe and whatever gear he was hauling.

The car started immediately and showed only a quarter-tank of gas. Jason ceremoniously looked back at the main house to vent his frustration. Little to no gas in his tank was a pet peeve he had that was mostly tied to his kids.

As he drove back toward the cabin, Jason looked at his surroundings again with a renewed appreciation of the forest and terrain. It always marveled him to think about the original Mr. Fox who appeared on the land by horse and wagon in the 1800's seeking his opportunity in farming. The tools they had were modest. Most of the work was by hand or supported by some other animal. It was not the easy Range Rover life his farm had morphed into today.

Callie heard the roll of tires come to a stop outside. She had just marinated the filets and left them on the stove to warm to room temperature. Zoe and Molly watched as Callie prepared dinner without a consideration to treat them. They could smell the warming meat that was now sitting above and out of sight on the stove.

After quickly washing her hands, Callie skipped to the front door to meet her man as he came home. As she pushed the screen door to welcome him, Jason was just stepping on to the wood platform that created the cottage's front stoop. She smiled as she greeted then looked behind him for her car.

"Where's my car?" she asked puzzled by what she saw.

"Oh," he mused to blow it off, "Clara misplaced the key fob. She'll bring it here when she finds it."

"Why would Clara have my key fob?"

Jason felt a panic grow within him. Callie did not know that he let Clara drive her car. It was also becoming obvious she also did not share his confidence in letting someone else drive her car.

"I let her drive it home from the shop when we picked up the Wagoneer," Jason confessed.

"You gave MY CAR to some woman I don't know to drive it back here?"

"Yes," he answered. "I'm sorry if that's a problem. I thought it was kind of a treat for her."

"Jesus Christ, Jason, that's my car. Not... a treat."

"Cal, I'm sorry," he answered. "I didn't think it was a big deal."

"Well, it is," she stated. "Lend her your car if you want to give her a treat."

Callie's intended message was not reflected in what she said. Her immediate thoughts went to Jason and Clara together in the pond. The *treat* could be inferred as something much more. He had already lent her his car.

Jason stood silently not knowing what to say. Callie began to cool as her eyes wandered from his to off into the trees then back onto his car.

"That's a mom car," she laughed knowing the insinuation would provoke him. "I had this car when the kids were little. Loved it. But we outgrew it."

Callie walked to the driver door to look inside. Jason could read on her saddening face the nostalgic thoughts of her kids as they were back then all buckled in for a ride somewhere. As she stood, she glossed her hand across the driver's side glass to finish her memory.

"Take you back?"

As she turned in silence, Callie looked as if she wanted to cry. The cars from her past that now aligned to the farm and to Jason's own primary transportation touched her too closely. She needed a supportive hug to assure her that everything was and was going to continue to be all right. Jason held her close until she decided to let go.

It took a few moments for Callie to collect her emotions as she separated from him. As she did, she made eye contact with a smile to reassure him that she was OK. Jason kept his right hand on her back as they walked back inside together. As they entered the living room, they found Zoe and Molly at the far end of the room looking to go out.

Jason and Callie parted as he went to address the needs of the dogs while Callie continued with her dinner preparation. As he opened the door and checked to see that the gate down to the woods was open, Callie meandered into the kitchen to check the meat temperature and to get some Rose'.

"Oh, for GOD'S SAKE!" she exclaimed

Jason turned quickly to her outcry to see what was wrong. As he looked to the kitchen, Callie appeared from a bent over position behind the counter holding the plate that had held their dinner.

The two scoundrels that had just eaten their meat had just made their get-away out the back door.

Jason held his breath to keep from laughing. Her response and frustration was amusing. He exhaled trying to think of their options. He checked his watch for the time to see what was possible. His watch read 4:30PM which meant he had missed the dinner order deadline for the cabins. But he knew the general store closed at 5PM. He had time to go there to replace their meal.

Jason quickly called Zoe back knowing Molly would follow. The two dogs appeared quickly but continued to maintain a safe distance.

"I'll go replace the meat," Jason declared. "Do you want to come?"

"No," Callie said in frustration. "I'll stay here with Thelma and Louise. I've had enough *country* for today."

Concern struck Jason as Callie's honesty came out unfiltered. He knew she was struggling with being there on top of all the other problems in her life. He decided to let the comment stand unanswered then left to rebuy dinner.

# # # #

Clara was walking out of the main house when she saw the Volvo accelerating hard out on to Blackburn Road. From the distance, the driver looked like Jason without either Zoe or Callie in the passenger seat. As she watched the car disappear into the trees, she looked at the key fob in her hand to reconsider returning the Range Rover now.

The overstuffed living room chair was perfect for Callie to relax with her Kindle to find an escape. She was just settling in to her story when she heard the grind of tires on the gravel outside. Knowing his out and back would take longer, she expected Jason to walk in having forgotten something. Chase had the same bad absent-mindedness when he had to run to the store.

"Hello?" called a familiar female voice.

When Callie looked up from her screen, she saw Clara leaning in through the front door. As their eyes met, Clara smiled and invited herself into the front hall to say hello.

"Hi Callie," Clara said loud enough to be heard across the room. "I have your car keys. I put your car right outside."

"Oh, thank you," Callie replied with a fake smile. "I appreciate you bringing it up. We would've come get it."

"No problem," Clara answered. "It's kind of a treat to drive."

Clara turned to leave as Callie stood. This was her opportunity to talk to Clara free of Jason. She wanted to get some answers to questions she would feel awkward asking him.

"Clara," Callie called out in a friendly tone, "Come in."

Clara paused before turning. The same desire to talk to Callie independent of Jason motivated her to return the Range Rover while he was gone.

"Got time for a glass of wine?"

Clara looked at her watch knowing that she had at least an hour before having to prepare baskets for guest dinners.

"I have time for one," she answered.

Callie uncorked a bottle of Rose that Jason had chilling in his bar cooler. The wine was familiar to her as one of her go-to's when home and needing some relief. Callie invited Clara to join her on the sofa that overlooked the deck and trees. As both nestled into their separate corner, each was thinking about how to pull information out of the other without surrendering too much on themselves.

"This property is fantastic," Callie opened to bait her line.

"Thank you. It was a dream my husband Tom and I had for years until we finally were able to do it."

Perfect, Callie thought as her mind went straight into recall when Clara mentioned Tom. She could visualize the photo of the two together on the website.

"Well, you've done a fabulous job," she answered. "I didn't quite know what to expect when I put this address in my GPS."

Callie gave a patronizing smile as Clara digested her comment. The words had a sting to them that were weaved into the compliment she could say she gave.

"I think our biggest challenge is marketing," Clara answered. "Jason has some great ideas."

Callie listened to her answer thinking about the simple logo on the gate post that marked the property on the road.

"I have a graphic design background if you need help," Callie added. "For example, I could help you update your logo into something that shines."

Callie loved the fact that she could demean something about the property that she knew she was able to improve. That Jason was active in the marketing made sense. He could place Fox Farms in all types of mediums that would generate interest and business. Callie's contributions would be the polishing of the final presentation.

"Oh," Clara replied with sadness.

She then moved uncomfortably to put her glass of wine on to the coffee table.

"Thank you," she continued but in a declarative manner. "But the logo, for as simple and pathetic as it is, was designed by my husband. So that can't change."

Callie noticed the sadness in Clara's voice as she took her stand. She then watched Clara regroup from the confrontation to pick her glass back up.

"I look forward to meeting him," Callie replied now digging for his whereabouts.

Clara took a sip of wine as she heard Callie's wish. She was beginning to piece together that Callie's questions were mining for information about the farm, Clara, and Tom. She began to feel nervous that her feelings for Jason were either obvious or, in some manner, discovered through Jason.

"Tom died early last fall," Clara finally answered. "He was sick with cancer for about a year. His expenses and the time away from this business were catastrophic."

Callie listened with compassion as Clara began to tell her story. She went through the history of her relationship with Tom during the time they met while both were working for Marriott. That romance included discussions of a property like Fox Farm long before they talked about getting married. Tom would often joke that he had married above his station; and, that Clara only married him to keep him from stealing her idea. He would tell people that she was the brains; and that he was the pack-mule.

When Clara got to the point of meeting Jason, she danced around his stay on Fox Farm during the Christmas and New Year's Holiday. The fact was that both of them were missing important elements of their families and Holiday traditions; and, that both were alone, went unmentioned. The totality of their relationship then was in passing as meals were delivered and directions were needed. A coincidental afternoon walk after New Year's Day placed them both on the fire trail to the back property at the same time. Clara walked with Jason to show him the mountain top.

"Jason has a way to pull information that you don't want to share right out of you," Clara stated as she looked to Callie for confirmation.

"Yes, he does," she answered recalling time with him on the deck overlooking the sand at his beach cottage. "You should meet his friend Rebecca."

Callie smiled at the image of Clara being softly interrogated by Rebecca without even knowing it.

"I've been warned," Clara answered. "Her family is coming to visit in a few weeks."

Callie readjusted her body to settle deeper into the cushions. Clara's story was fascinating and not terribly unlike hers. Her husband's departure was severe and fast similar to her divorce from Chase. The only difference was that Callie and Chase had hope and resources to get through it. Clara was left with the same emptiness piled on with the potential to lose her dream and livelihood.

"Then Jason's a *'white knight'* for both us." Callie stated to disclose her knowledge of his ownership.

Clara's heart sank that Callie knew that fact. That Jason disclosed his ownership was not surprise. It just made her sad that she knew it and had a feeling of power through it.

"He did save the day," Clara reflected. "And the farm, for that matter."

"From the looks of things, you two get along swimmingly."

Clara's sadness jumped with the sarcastic accusation that there was something more to her relationship with her boss. She began to think about the unexpected pond swim with glee now that she knew it was bothering Callie. But she also knew she could not rub it back into her face. She had to be tactful.

"Callie," she answered quietly and calmly. "We're friends. He's my boss. But we're just friends too."

Callie got no satisfaction from Clara's declaration. She read her tone as a snarky, in-your-face declaration of game-on through distraction. Callie studied Clara's expression as she leaned forward with her glass to toast.

"To Fox Farm and your combined success," Callie said to throw down the gauntlet.

Clara smiled as she extended her glass to touch Callie's. As each took their celebratory drink, the front door wisped open.

"I'm back," Jason declared nervously. "I see Clara brought your car back. What else did I miss?"

13

Lizzie returned to her room after another disappointing dinner with her dad and brother Will. The clock on her nightstand read 8PM. She looked out into the glow of dusk knowing that if she were either home, in Asheville, or at the beach with her mom, life would be more fun.

After trying unsuccessfully to reach her friends to Facetime, Lizzie resorted to her go-to knowing that her mom was likely out at dinner somewhere nice having a good time without her. She expected that her grandmother Carolyn would be done with dinner and likely watching Netflix.

The sound of the call rose from her phone as she stared at her grandmother's picture on the screen. As usual, Gram was not answering as quickly as most people. Lizzie knew it would take a few more cycles before Gram would tune in to the sound, find her iPad, and answer her call.

After the fifth try, Lizzie became irritated that Gram did not answer. She closed out the Facetime app and went to Tik Tok for entertainment. She decided to call Gram in the morning.

Jason laughed as he removed their plates from the outdoor table. The night was dark around them with the glow of citronella candles as their only light. Nothing else could be seen except for the moon that was hidden by the trees that filtered its light back through. The air was still, warm, and lovely. Callie loved this aspect of being in the mountains.

As Jason sat down, he refilled Callie's glass with the second bottle of Rose'. There was an awkward sense in the air when he arrived to find her with Clara. His questions then and through dinner gave no insight to their discussion. They were congenial. So, in his mind, that was a win.

"I'm not so sure I should have this," Callie said as she gave Jason a playful look. "I'm half your weight and way ahead of you."

Jason smiled at the insinuation. With it only being their second night together, he remained concerned about moving too fast. Maybe sedating Callie with more Rose' was the easiest solution to his dilemma.

"So…. Clara's story's a sad one," Callie stated to start mining him for information.

"Yes," he answered. "I showed up about six months after her husband died and about six months before her business was going to die too."

"You're everyone's White Knight, Jason Cartwright."

"It's an investment Callie, not charity."

"Why did you buy the whole thing? Wouldn't it have been better… more benevolent?… just to have just invested as a part ownership?"

The question seemed fair. Callie's dad always advocated shared risk. Her recent months of watching Shark Tank confirmed that thinking as modern. Jason took a moment to think. Callie's astute observation was asking for more than just a business answer he did not want to address.

"The amount needed was too large… And I require a certain return on investment. Quite frankly, she did not want any charity. She's a smart woman and wanted a business deal that worked for her and for me."

"So, she got out whole financially and has employment for life."

Callie's tone was notably sarcastic and bothered Jason.

"No," he answered with disdain. "She sold for a price that made her whole, gave her a nest-egg, a job for as long as it works for both of us, AND one of the three lots on top of the mountain. Her husband's ashes are scattered there. She did that after our deal closed and her future was secured."

Not sensing Jason's dislike for her insinuations, Callie took a large swallow of Rose' to think through Clara's permanence on the farm. From the story she told, she would never leave where Tom's ashes were spread. And, with her ownership of a lot on top of the mountain where Jason wants to build a house, Clara was going to remain in view whether as an employee or not. The compounding of those two facts made her anxious.

"I'm sorry," Callie admitted. "I'm a lot tipsy and am having a hard time with this reconnection thing. I guess I'm a little jealous."

"I get it. Your ability to trust anyone is shot."

Callie exhaled through her smile as she leaned to kiss him.

"I trust you Jason Cartwright," she whispered.

"Then let's toast to that."

# # # #

As Jason finished the dinner dishes, Callie curled-up on the sofa in the living room. She floated in its soft cushions as the air conditioning cooled her skin from the day's heat and humidity. Jason watched her for movement as he dried his hands with a dish towel then set hung it on the rack to dry. Callie looked out for the count.

To not disturb her, he walked to the deck to blow out the candles. He sent the dogs down the stairs to the tree line to do their business before coming in for the night. As he waited, he could hear a vibration coming from inside the house. He checked his pocket for his phone then looked inside to Callie's. Her phone was lit and moving on the coffee table.

Curiosity overcame good sense as Jason quickly moved to wake Callie to answer her phone. As he entered the room, he saw PATTY written on the phone screen. Her oldest sister was calling.

"Hello," Jason answered.

"Who's this?" Patty answered in a hurried voice.

"It's Jason… Jason Cartwright Patty. How are you?"

"Where's Callie? I NEED TO SPEAK TO HER."

Patty's voice was panicked. From their first words, Jason had worked his way to the couch to shake Callie awake. As she looked at Jason through her groggy state, his expression and the phone in her face said something was wrong.

"It's Patty."

Callie fought the cushions to sit up and take the phone.

"Patty?" Callie said in a grumbled voice. "What's wrong?"

"Mom's had a stroke or something. We're heading there now. Where the hell are you!?"

"I'm in Asheville, Asheville North Carolina. Chase is in Nantuck…"

"Jesus, Callie. Could you be any further away? We'll be there in two hours. You need to get there as fast as you can."

"Ok, ok. I'll leave now."

Callie hung up the phone. Her information was sketchy. What she was not told is that that her mother was discovered by a visiting friend unconscious in her front hallway. She was then taken to the hospital in Williamsburg. The expectation was that Carolyn would stay there unless transferred to a higher-level hospital, if needed.

"I have to go," Callie declared as she wobbled to stand.

"Go where?"

"Williamsburg. My mom.... my mom..."

Callie broke into tears as Jason moved to catch her collapsing body. He sat them both on the couch to get more information. Callie was in no condition to drive anywhere.

"I'll drive you," Jason commanded. "Let's get our things packed and go."

Packing took little time since Callie had not unpacked beyond her hanging bag. Jason's bad habit of cycling clothes through his suitcase and laundry basket paid off for a quick getaway.

The Range Rover was loaded quickly as both dogs jumped into the back seat. Callie was functioning but remained an emotional wreck. As they drove down the lane from the *Flying Dutchman*, Jason turned toward the Main house that still had its lights on. Clara was reading to relax in one of the drawing rooms when she saw the headlights wash through the room from the window. Sensing something was wrong, she met the car at the kitchen door. Jason was already unloading Zoe as Clara walked down the grass.

"Everything OK?" she asked.

"No, I need you to take care of Zoe for a few days. I'm taking Callie to Williamsburg. Her mom was just taken to the hospital."

The urgency of sudden hospital evacuations was familiar to Clara from Tom's decline. She grabbed Zoe's collar to keep her from following Jason back to the car.

"Thank you so much. I'll text you information as I can. Her food is at the Dutchman."

"Don't worry about Zoe," Clara replied as he turned back to the car. "JASON. Please be careful."

Jason paused then turned back to give her a reassuring smile and touch on her arm for comfort. Within seconds, the black Range Rover was rolling down the driveway and was roaring off into the darkness on Blackburn Road.

Clara's only sight of Callie was to see her distraught in the glow of the Range Rover's interior lamps looking off into the night. She knew the pain she was feeling. To say anything to her would have been counterproductive. Clara also knew Jason likely had some alcohol in him from dinner. Afraid for them, for him, she looked up to the clear night sky littered with the stars she always felt she could touch to ask God that they both arrive safely.

14

"I have to call the kids," was the first thing Callie said as Jason merged from the country road onto the interstate heading east. "They'll want to know what's going on."

"You really don't know much, Callie," Jason responded worried her children would have questions she could not answer.

"Siri, call Chase."

The voice command on her iPhone activated and appeared on the dashboard screen. An English male voice confirmed the call being placed to Chase. Jason found it funny that Callie's Siri voice would be male and British. His was an Australian woman.

The phone rang several times before a text appeared back on the screen.

I am sorry I cannot take your call right now.

Callie was familiar with the one-touch response for unwanted calls. She had used it countless times on him as he tried to reach her through the course of the year.

"Siri, text Chase," she commanded.

Callie's head was bobbing as she watched the dashboard screen.

"What you like to say to Chase?" her male Brit Siri asked.

"Mom has been taken to the hospital. Period. I'm on my way there now. Period. I don't know anything else. Period. Please tell kids..... Period."

Jason kept one eye on the highway as he watched her words appear on the screen. A few words were misinterpreted. But enough were intact that the message and urgency would be clear.

"Maybe he'll answer now," she said before angrily whispering. *"Asshole."*

As she turned to look back out her window, her phone sounded with the Guess Who's *No Time Left for You* ringtone. Being a seventies rocker, Jason was familiar with the song as a send-off to something that was the past to move on to better things. He knew Callie was more of a disco fan from that era preferring the Bee Gee's to anything else. The song must have connected to Chase in more ways than just the divorce. Callie pushed the answer button on the screen to connect with him.

"Callie, your message was scrambled. What's going on?" asked the voice that was familiar to both of them.

"Mom has had a stroke…. we think. Patty's on her way now. We'll know more once she gets there."

"Well, where are you?" he asked. "I thought you were there?"

Callie looked to Jason. Her face showed panic as both heard the question.

"I was in Asheville near the Biltmore that we saw with the kids."

"I know the Biltmore, Callie," he answered. "It's almost 10 o'clock. How are you getting to Williamsburg?"

"I'm driving right now. I'll be there around…"

Jason held up three fingers to indicate 3 AM.

"3 AM," she finished.

"Jesus Christ, Callie. You won't be able to do anything at that time of night. You should have waited and flown in the morning."

"Just tell the kids what's going on. Call Michael. Or wait until he's up. He's six hours ahead."

Chase ran his fingers through his hair as he pondered telling his kids. Will was out with his friends. Lizzie was huddled up in her room likely on Facetime with her friends from home.

"I'll tell them. Please be careful and stop. Not getting there is worse than being a few hours late."

Jason saw Callie smile in appreciation of his comment. 3 AM was an aggressive ETA. He was hopeful she would be able to sleep while they drove.

The end of the call was sterile. After they disconnected, Callie fell into thought about the timing of her mother's stroke and the stress her divorce may have added to cause it. Her face winced in pain as tears streamed down her cheeks. Jason moved his right hand to her shoulder to offer his love and support while continuing to drive eighty miles per hour with his left hand and knee. The width of the center console between them made his touch less than what she needed.

"Callie, get some sleep," he said as he rubbed her shoulder. "Patty will call with news when she gets there. I'll wake you up."

Callie looked at him with just a helpless, forced smile. She then quietly curled up against the door to fall asleep.

# # # #

Chase found what he expected when he reached the top of the stairs. Lizzie's door was closed. The light that leaked through the gap at the bottom told him that she was still awake. As he approached to knock, he stopped to listen. Lizzie was talking to someone. The responding voice was older and male. She was Facetiming with her oldest brother, Michael.

"Lizzie," Chase called out as he knocked on her door.

The conversation in the room went silent as Chase opened her door. Lizzie was laying on her bed with her iPhone propped against the lamp on her nightstand. Her head was laying comfortably on her pillow beside it.

Lizzie reached for her phone as Chase entered. She spun its face toward her dad to show Michael on the other end. Michael visited for Christmas as the family was finishing its counseling. After he left to return to Madrid, Chase started traveling again and all the counseling ended. This was their first face-to-face since then. His face showed the disdain Chase expected.

"I've got nothing to say to you," Michael said as he reached to cut the call.

"Your grandmother," Chase choked out. "Your grandmother has had a stroke and is in the hospital."

Michael's face held still as Lizzie sat up in her bed.

"I tried to Facetime her today," Lizzie cried. "Is she going to be OK?"

"We don't know. Aunt Patty is on her way. Your mom is heading there too. I'll let you know as you know as I know things."

Chase sat down next to Lizzie as she struggled to comprehend what was happening. Carolyn was, in many ways, an extension of Callie to her. Lizzie always enjoyed visiting her Gram for everything they did together except gardening.

"Thanks for letting me know, Dad," Michael said in a cold tone.

"I'm sure we'll know more in the morning." Chase replied.

Chase put his hand on Lizzie's shoulder to comfort her. As her emotions finally released, Lizzie jumped toward her dad for a supporting hug. Her arms closed around him pressing the face of her phone against his back. Moments later, when she looked again for Michael, he was gone.

"I want to be in Williamsburg," Lizzie declared.

"Aunt Patty and mom will be there to keep us updated," Chase replied.

"What if she dies?" Callie cried.

As Chase reached to hug his child again, the need for her to be there became urgent. He decided to research every form of travel to get Lizzie and Will to Williamsburg in the morning.

# # # #

Callie woke as Jason exited the interstate for gas and caffeine. She grabbed only water to hydrate knowing that anything else with either sugar or caffeine would keep her up. Jason grabbed his go-to twenty-four-ounce Mountain Dew for its high-octane caffeine and sugar. It was a drink he liked but would pass-by for diet sodas to stay thin.

The Range Rover had just returned to Interstate 40 East near Winston-Salem when Callie's phone shifted from the acoustic play list Jason wanted to Cindy Lauper's *Girls just want to have fun*. Jason guessed correctly that the caller was Patty. The dash display lit to confirm his guess.

"Patty?" Callie asked. "How's mom?"

"It's not good," Patty replied.

Callie's expression and shoulders dropped with the Patty's assessment. The doctors painted a grim picture of the time that had lapsed between the stroke and her time of discovery. Carolyn was resting comfortably as more tests and scans were being scheduled to make a final diagnosis. Patty told Callie that she did visit Carolyn briefly who was breathing on her own but unconscious.

"We'll know more in the morning," was how Patty ended her news.

Callie stayed silent as the updated information sank in. Jason chose not to talk to not stir any ill feelings Patty may still have had toward him from twenty-eight years ago. Callie's silence lasted too long to not say anything to close the call.

"Patty," he said. "It's Jason. We just passed Winston-Salem. We should arrive as expected. Are you staying there?"

"Oh, I'm glad you're with her," Patty answered. "We're going back to mom's to check the house and to get some sleep. You should just go there."

"Ok, I'll get the address from Cal and put it in the GPS."

"Thanks, Jason.... Really. Thank you for being there."

The Spotify playlist returned after Patty disconnected playing Eric Clapton's *Change the World*. Callie's face was still withdrawn as she struggled with her thoughts.

"The last thing I said to my mother was to mind her own business," she whispered toward the floor.

Jason's reach to comfort her got no response. He needed to convince her to go back to sleep. She needed to be rested to face what was coming in the morning. Sleep would get her there faster.

"Callie, you need to sleep. You can fix all of that tomorrow, face-to-face, when you see her."

Jason's words of comfort seemed to work as Callie again curled up against the door to fall asleep again.

# # # #

Chase opened his laptop with the initial thought to get Lizzie and Will to Williamsburg by plane. He figured the flying time would be about three hours. With getting to the airport, security advance time, flight time, and layovers, he expected the entire trip to take about eight hours. He surveyed the available flights leaving from Nantucket for the first available flights. He then checked Delta airlines for both flights and connecting flights in order to use his frequent flyer miles.

The first flight leaving the island that he knew they could comfortably make was at 11AM. It flew through JFK in New York City then to Dulles with a finishing regional leg to Williamsburg. Their expected arrival time was 6PM if everything worked as planned. From there, they could either Uber or Lyft to find Callie and to be with their grandmother.

The timing of Carolyn's stroke was troubling. Despite all the recent nastiness that erupted in the divorce, Chase always had a loving relationship with Callie's mom and dad. He was accepted into the family without hesitation. He golfed regularly with Callie's dad. It was difficult for him to think about Carolyn in dire circumstances and his soon-to-be ex-wife having to deal with that and incoming children at the same time.

As the arrow hovered over the purchase button for the flights, Chase paused to revisit his past with Callie's family. He opened a new window on his laptop to check the ferry schedule back to Hyannis. The first departure from Nantucket was at 8AM.

15

The landscaping lights illuminated the front of the house as Jason pulled the Range Rover up to the front door of Carolyn's home. The house was more impressive than the Google street view he admitted to Callie that he saw when he snooped on her life over the years. Her parents were friends of his parents even after their engagement broke. Knowing where they landed when they moved from Pittsburgh to Williamsburg twenty years ago was easy to uncover.

Jason parked behind what he assumed was Patty's Mercedes E350, 4-matic station wagon. Callie stirred as he shifted into park and Molly began to sense the end of their trip. Callie looked to see where she was then opened the door without comment. She unloaded Molly and headed straight to the front door. Jason hurried to unload her suitcase and his bag to follow.

As they entered Carolyn's home, Callie proceeded to the stairs. She was halfway to the second floor when she noticed Jason did not follow her.

"Jason, I'm too tired. You're with me tonight."

Jason felt uncomfortable with the thought of sleeping in one her parent's bedrooms with Callie while her mother was not there. It was eerily similar to some sleepovers he had with her twenty-eight years ago when her parents traveled. He slowly proceeded up the stairs uncertain what would be waiting in the morning when he would see Patty for the first time since the engagement broke.

Callie was in the bedroom's dedicated bathroom when he entered with their bags. As she finished, Jason dug into his bag for his shaving kit then waited for her exit. He took his time through the bathroom to void his bladder and to brush his teeth. When he returned to the room, he found what expected. Callie was already in bed and asleep. Still a little wired from his long, Mountain Dew enhanced, drive, Jason gently sat on the side of the bed to watch her sleep. Her breathing was quiet as her body sat motionless. Despite all the turmoil, her appearance was perfect. Jason kissed her lightly on the cheek before crawling in beside her.

# # # #

The blinds were open bringing early light into the room with the sunrise. Both Jason and Callie were early risers who liked to sleep with their blinds open to let the sunshine gently welcome them back for the new day.

As he woke, Jason looked around for his first full-light impression of the room. It had the beautiful appointments that he expected. Callie was already up and gone. There were no sounds coming from the bathroom. She had to be downstairs.

As he sat up in bed, he ran his hand across the sheets and comforter. His first thought was to wonder if this was the bed where Callie and Chase would sleep, cuddle, and make love when they were visiting. The thought angered him. Not that she did it; but that he was why it happened. If Jason had married Callie as planned, he would have been with her all those years to sleep with her in this bed.

As he walked to the bathroom, he put his shorts back on to be properly attired to go downstairs. He did a quick brush of his hair with minimal satisfaction. A few alfalfa sprouts required some water. He then brushed his teeth to ensure his breath was in good shape to meet Patty again. He could hear voices coming from the kitchen as he descended the stairs. He recognized both of them.

Before entering the kitchen, Jason stopped to listen to the tone of the conversation. The conversation was light, casual and included a few laughs. He felt safe to walk in.

Callie was standing next to the kitchen island with her back to him while her sister Patty sat on a stool that faced him. They continued to talk as each took pulls from their coffee mugs adorned in flowers. Patty noticed Jason as he appeared from around the corner. Her eyes shifted as her face remained still. She pinched her lips to hold her smile as Callie continued talking to finish her point. As Jason put his hand on her shoulder, Callie jumped startled by the unexpected touch.

"Good morning," he said first to get it out of the way.

Callie recovered from her surprise with a laugh then instinctively kissed him on the lips to say good morning. The gesture surprised both him and Patty whose eyes opened widely. Jason's stiff response bothered Callie who laughed.

"She knows we slept together last night," Callie said. "No sex yet though. She also knows the whole story from last fall."

Callie's reference back to last fall made Jason uncomfortable. Her visit that started to just snoop from afar changed when she chased him down at the gas station where they coincidentally both stopped. Callie was livid and emotionally weak when Chase chose a boys' golf weekend over her. Her weekend with Jason almost ended with them making love when he stopped them. Chase discovered and caught her with Jason as she was leaving. That fall weekend cut open their marriage for the examination that led to their pending divorce. Callie's confession of the entire weekend to Patty changed her opinion of Jason. He was no longer the devil.

"Patty." Jason said to greet her while still embarrassed by the kiss.

"Hi Jason," Patty replied with a grin. "You've aged well."

Jason laughed at the remark and responded with his usual "ditto". Callie then placed a filled coffee mug in front of him along with a china sugar bowl and creamer.

The update they had on Carolyn was no change. She had slept through the night and was still sleeping comfortably. Callie and Patty had time to shower and dress before heading over to see her. Jason's plan was to remain at Carolyn's home to be where and how needed.

# # # #

The nurse that answered Patty's early morning call recommended a family member be in Carolyn's room by 9AM when the doctors rounded with news and plans for the day. The two sisters left in Patty's Mercedes to be there fifteen minutes before nine. Before leaving, Callie insisted that Jason stay behind to make any calls to his kids, Fox Farm or anywhere else that needed his attention. Both she and her sister expected that the day would be long. Jason agreed to check-in periodically with texts and to visit with them for lunch around noon.

Being left alone in Carolyn's house gave Jason opportunity to take a self-tour. As he walked the first floor, a lot of the furnishings and art he saw were familiar. As he studied the living room, he noticed an oil painting above the fireplace that he remembered from their Pittsburgh home. Callie's dad gave him its impressive history up to the point he bought it using his first, ever, bonus check.

The sunroom resembled their Pittsburgh home with lots of glass overlooking the backyard and James River. The leather couch appeared to be the same one he sat on when he asked her dad for Callie's hand in marriage. He could see her dad sitting in the matching chair now as he did then.

As he made his way through the first floor, he did a headcount of bedrooms. The master was off the first-floor family room. The upstairs had no more than three bedrooms with dedicated bathrooms. The thought of holidays in the house created a picture of grandchildren packed in rooms with their parents as the three sisters, their spouses, and kids all came together. The visualization of the resulting congestion did not suit either Callie or her sisters.

Jason returned to the kitchen where he found the stairs to the basement. He remembered a traditional pool table with leather strap pockets in their Pittsburgh house. It was a source of fun for him and Callie when they started dating. He knew her dad would not have left it behind in the move.

As he reached the bottom of the basement stairs, he found the game room he expected complete with the pool table he remembered, a monster television, and a comfortable sectional couch. This is where the kids were sent when the adults wanted their my-time. To the left of the stairs was a slatted door to a small laundry and utility room that hosted the constant-flow hot water heater, furnace, and air conditioning air handler.

Beyond the couch, Jason noticed two doors located next to each other. A quick look showed bunk beds in one and matching bunk beds with a crib and changing table in the other. The house was perfect for family visits just as he expected it to be.

Jason returned to the bedroom to shower and dress for the day. The bed was unmade which was the one thing he always tended to before starting his day. In his opinion, there was nothing worse than finding the bed unmade at bedtime. As he finished, he fluffed Calle's pillow which released a perfume scent that was her. The smell instilled in him a feeling of completeness he could never describe or explain. He brought his face in to savor its scent. For a moment, the tragedy unfolding with Carolyn left his consciousness.

It was 9:30 when Jason returned to the front hall where Carolyn was found. As that thought entered his mind, he stopped to look around. There nothing he could see that showed anything traumatic had happened in the room. It was as clean, elegant, and sterile as he would have expected it to be if visiting. Sadness filled him as he looked around at Carolyn's life that evolved after him without the pleasure of her company to have given him a proper tour.

# # # #

Callie's update was promising but still not good. Her mother was awake when they arrived but confused about what happened and how she got there. Callie started to cry when she talked about the notable slur in her speech along with paralysis on her left side. The doctor's initial assessment was that the debilitation was likely permanent. But there was always hope.

"I know it was wrong. But I absolutely fell apart when I saw her," Callie confessed to him.

Jason understood the struggle she had when first seeing her life's touchstone, her rock, lying crippled in a hospital bed.

"I know it's hard," Jason empathized. "Your mom knows how deeply you love her. Your emotions show that."

Callie heard the words but missed what he was trying to say. Her last conversation with her mother followed by the childish meltdown that just occurred was selfish.

"Up until now," she cried, "my last words to her were *to stay out of my business.*"

Jason's eye's welled with tears as he heard the pain she was feeling.

"Kids say the harshest things to their parents that seem right at the time but are fully regrettable when they get time to think about it. I have done it. My kids do it. Your kids likely have done. And, I know in your history with your mom and dad, you have done it."

Callie smiled through her tears to the truth she was hearing. She immediately recalled several incidents in high school and one particularly rough, *get-over-it* conversation she had with her dad when she broke her engagement with Jason. The F-bomb dropped then and did not get a pass. The thought of that moment helped bring some peace to her pain.

"My mom said she understood why I said what I did."

"Your mom gets you, and loves you, more than life. Be there for her now."

Callie exhaled in relief as she was beginning to feel better through her conversation with Jason. His ability to bring her back to earth when things were dire continued to be there for her. They agreed on a time for lunch before both said *love you* then disconnected.

# # # #

With two hours to kill before meeting Callie for lunch, Jason decided to drive through Williamsburg to revisit the soccer fields where he watched his kids play in the Jefferson Cup Tournaments. He also mapped a drive through the College of William and Mary and by historic Williamsburg to get some air. He was surprised by how well he remembered the area and how to get from place to place. He recalled always being excited, and fearful, to be there knowing he could run into either Callie or her mother at any moment.

As Jason drove past a massive, historic, Catholic Church with adjoining cemetery, he thought about Callie's dad's obituary that he saw online. The *St. James* name sounded familiar. When he Googled her father's name, his obituary reappeared topped by the face he remembered. His recollection was correct that her dad was buried somewhere in the cemetery. He had time to visit the gravesite and pulled in to find him.

The person in the church office was immensely helpful when Jason asked for directions. His story included his history with the family minus the problems that erupted with the engagement and cancelled wedding. He was given a map that marked his current location. An X was placed in the area where Callie's dad was laid to rest. The woman said it had a lovely view.

Jason drove the Range Rover back into the cemetery on its winding, single lane road. From his own experience with his parents, he recalled the confusion he had in their cemetery in Pittsburgh as roads intersected and wound about without any directional signs to help. During his first return to visit his dad's grave, Jason got lost and drove several miles of winding, single-lane road to reach a gravesite that was only several hundred yards from the cemetery's main entrance. After that experience, he started noting and using markers that included family mausoleums and one distinctly odd pyramid shaped headstone to find his parents.

The thought of being buried frightened Jason. He told his children that he wanted to be cremated then dropped offshore from the beach house. That would make it easy for them to talk to him anytime they visited. If they wanted to know what he was thinking, he told them they could cast a line into the water. Whatever they would reel back in would be his answer. As he expected, only he found that funny. And with the mountain property, he was rethinking the ocean to the pond.

Jason parked the Range Rover where the woman in the office said would provide the easiest path up to the family plot. The spacing of the graves showed that this was not a pauper's cemetery. As he reached the crown of the hill, he saw Callie's dad's headstone. It was a simple, classic granite stone. In front of it was a well-tended row of flowers. A white, cast iron bend sat just off to the left. Jason looked to the surroundings. The woman was right. It was an extraordinary place to spend eternity.

Jason was emotionless until he saw the headstone. He took a moment to admire the setting that was so fitting for the man that gave his permission to Jason to marry his daughter.

"I bet you can't believe I'm standing here," Jason said, uncertain if it was proper. "Fact is, I can't either."

The words were coming easily. His faith wondered if her dad was listening. But he had to finish the one thing he always wanted to say to him.

"I'm sorry big guy," Jason said as he walked to the base of the grave. "God set me up with the most beautiful woman who loved me, who I adored like no other, and who had a family, like mine, that was so supportive and willing to help me succeed. And, I turned my back on it. I.... fucked... up. And you did not clobber me for that. Thank you."

Jason could feel tears welling in his eyes as he struggled with the last few word. He looked off to collect himself as if embarrassed to be in front of her dad.

"I'll do what's right for her," he finished. "She before me. I promise you that."

Jason circled around the gravesite to touch the headstone. He reached into his pocket to find a metal golf ball marker with their Pittsburgh golf club's logo on it. Jason had several in his shaving bag from trips taken with family and friends. Something told him to grab one this morning. He thought it was from the nostalgia of being in Carolyn's home. He knelt to place the marker on the small ledge at the base of the headstone.

As he moved to leave the gravesite, he touched her dad's headstone one last time. He then washed his hand across the white, cast iron bench where, he knew, Carolyn would sit to visit after tending to the flowers.

Jason left the hilltop with a renewed spirit. When he checked the time, he saw he had less than thirty minutes to get to the hospital to meet Callie and Patty for lunch. He looked back as he walked down the hill to see the headstone with the golf ball marker slowly disappear from sight. The rejuvenation that had built through his visit began to fade to sadness. He needed to find Callie.

16

The hospital corridor was dimly lit by fluorescent light and littered with computer carts, gurney beds, and food service lunch wagons. The sight reminded him of the last months of his dad's life when he would spend consecutive days visiting as his father continued to fight his body's collapse.

As Jason approached Carolyn's room, he stopped to think about whether the sight of him would be helpful or hurtful. Callie gave no instructions other than the time to meet and her mom's room number. Jason sent a text to let her know he was in the hallway.

"She's resting," Callie said as she emerged from the room in front of him.

There was no hesitation to kiss and embrace. They had the same need to touch each other.

"I didn't know how she'd react to seeing me. I didn't want to add any stress."

Callie smiled as she listened. She had the same concern but chose not to verbalize it to either Jason or to Patty.

"Let's go. I'm starving. Patty is staying here for when she wakes up."

As they turned to head to the elevator, Jason placed his arm around Callie's shoulder to give her a second embrace. He was surprised when she sidestepped away slightly to let his arm fall. Her grab of his hand was firm and more comfortable to reestablish contact.

As the elevator door closed to complete privacy, Callie released Jason's hand to cover her face with hers.

"She's not going to get better," she cried.

Jason's first inclination was to encourage her with *it's going to be fine*. But he knew from his own experience with his parents that final declines usually start with a trigger event that opens doors for other things to pile on to. A stroke to a woman in her eighties was such an event.

"I'm so sorry Cal,"

"This is such a game-changer. I should've seen it coming. I mean, she's eighty-four years old."

"Have faith."

Jason felt his remark to hold faith would be uplifting. Callie's Catholic upbringing that went casual for a few decades reignited when she had children and solidified when her dad died. She looked to God for answers for his sickness and was devastated when he lost his battle with cancer. Right now, her faith was failing instead of helping her.

"You say that when you have none yourself," she replied.

"I have faith that things will work out regardless of the outcome. You are a strong woman with a strong family. You're blessed in so many ways. Everything will be fine."

"I wish I could share your optimism"

"I'm here for you for whatever you need me to do."

Callie stared at the floor as his words floated past her. Her thoughts migrated to what was to come with her mother's needs and care. How could all of that be addressed with Patty in the D.C. area and her other sister, Maggie, in California. Callie had the most flexibility of the three without either a career or family to anchor her anywhere. She began to feel the full weight of the situation build upon her shoulders.

"Tell me you mean that," Callie replied.

"I MEAN THAT, I'm here for you."

Callie retook Jason's hand as the elevator door opened to cafeteria. After a quick survey of the place and the food offered, they both agreed that a drive to get a good meal with better aesthetics and fresh air was better than a quick dine in the hospital cafeteria.

# # # #

Carolyn was awake when Callie and Jason returned to the floor. Although still weak, she had limited capacity to process conversation and to show expressions. The doctors assured Patty that Carolyn could hear and process what they were saying. She was fully aware of what she was now facing. Her fear, however, was not for herself. It was for her children.

Jason stayed in a small waiting room as Callie returned to visit with her mother. Patty was eager to take some time away to check in with her family and to find something to eat. Callie shared their impression of the cafeteria's offering along with directions to a nearby strip mall that hosted a variety of take-out options. Patty waved to Jason as she passed by the waiting room then disappeared.

Jason checked his phone for any messages as something to do. He did not expect anything pressing except for maybe some sister complaints from his kids or a need from Clara. As he opened his text messages, he saw one from Clara and one from Faith. He opened Clara's first.

I hope you made it safely and that things are fine with Callie's mom. Let me know on both. Zoe misses you. She paced around all night.

Jason replied with a smile emoji then asked Clara to give Zoe a hug for him. He did not have any idea on when he would be back. But he thought a week was a good window to expect. Clara responded promptly as if waiting.

She'll be fine. She's in the best place in the world.

Jason smiled at the words as he envisioned his brownie on the front lawn chasing the geese away from the pond. He felt bad that Clara would have to deal with the swims that often took place afterwards that required a good hosing and scrub to remove the pond smell and debris.

Faith's text was to inquire when Jason expected to return to the cottage. They were running low on cash and no one wanted to use their credit cards to buy for the others.

Use the card I gave you. I'm now in Williamsburg with Callie. Her mom is in the hospital. I'd like to have someone come bring me a car so I can commute back and forth if needed. The wrangler is fine.

Jason looked at the time on his phone as he sent the message. It was approaching 3PM which meant that the Jeep delivery would likely be tomorrow. He sat back in contemplation of another night in Carolyn's house. His concern was that Callie's highly emotional state and need for loving support would lead her to want something from him that should wait for a happier moment in time. He opened the Trivago app on his phone to see what hotel options were available.

"My mom wants to see you," Callie said surprising him away from his room search.

As he instinctively stood, he intentionally angled his screen away to keep Callie from seeing what he was doing.

"You told her I was here?"

"No, she remembered I was with you," Callie replied with a smile. "She knew you would be here."

Jason smiled to both her absolute expectation and to the fact that Carolyn's mental faculties seemed to be in good shape. As they walked to the room, Callie painted a picture what he should expect. The always put-together woman he remembered was twenty-four hours into her stroke and hospital ordeal. There was nothing to either primp or prep her for visitors.

That comment amused Jason until Callie finished her staging to expect her voice to be weak and that the left side of her body and face were paralyzed.

Carolyn's bed was propped up to give her a sense of sitting for both comfort and conversation. She was facing the door as Callie led Jason into the room. A smile showed on the side of her face that still moved. As she watched them both near, Carolyn's thoughts returned to happier times in Pittsburgh when Jason and Callie dated. Because of the divorce, Carolyn was delighted to hear Jason's story of renewed love for her youngest daughter. And although she still hoped Callie's marriage and family would rebound, she found comfort in the option Callie had with Jason.

Jason's heart sank when he first looked at Carolyn. She was a beautiful, older version of what he remembered despite having tussled hair and wearing no make-up. To him, she was always an elegant, distinguished woman with both grace and style. As he would tell his daughters often, *"the apple never falls far from the tree".* Callie was truly her mother. His kids also showed clear traits of being both Jason and his ex-wife Stephanie. Some good. And, some not-so-good.

"Thank you for being here for Callie," Carolyn struggled to say with a heavy slur.

"I'm sorry to be here under these circumstances," Jason replied. "It would have been much nicer to have our first visit be in your lovely garden."

Carolyn smiled to the sentiment as she reached her right hand for his. Her hand felt like a small pouch of sticks as her weak grip took hold. She then shook his hand modestly as she smiled not taking her eyes off his.

"Whatever you need Carolyn," Jason added. "Just ask."

Carolyn's eyes shifted to Callie who was standing at the foot of the bed. Callie's eyes were puffy and red as she wiped away her tears. Carolyn returned to see Jason still there holding her hand.

She then closed her eyes to sleep now comfortable that her main worry had the support she needed.

Jason felt Carolyn's grip subside as her eyes closed. He looked to the monitors to find hope. Although weak and slow, Carolyn's pulse continued as she took breaths with ease.

"She does that," Callie added. "She'll sleep for a while."

Jason placed Carolyn's arm next to her side. He touched the top of her hand as he stepped back watching his former, future mother-in-law rest peacefully.

"What am I going to do?" Callie asked.

"The best you can," he answered. "But wait until you talk to the doctors and Patty, and Maggie, when she arrives."

# # # #

Jason stayed in the room with Callie as Carolyn continued to sleep. Callie filled the time lost in her phone which he knew would annoy her if she were Lizzie. The time was approaching 5PM which meant a need to find dinner. Patty did not return as expected. The pressure was too much for her too. She took some extra time to find peace in the gardens of Historic Williamsburg. Jason sat quietly watching Carolyn sleep while periodically checking her vitals on the electronic monitor above her bed. He had a numbness in him he remembered feeling when he was in his parent's hospital rooms under similar circumstances. It was a bad feeling.

The vibration of his phone in his pocket announced a text from somewhere. When he checked his phone, he discovered it was a message from Faith.

> *Can we bring the wrangler tomorrow? The guys are here and no one will leave with me.*

Jason's first thought amused him. *I don't know, can you?* was his typical response to grammatically deficient requests like this. He decided to spare Faith his need to amuse himself.

That's fine. Text me your ETA. I'll tell you where to meet me.

His reply received immediate *thumbs up* and *smile* emojis. Jason knew that Faith likely misrepresented who really did not want to leave the boys with her sisters.

As Jason shifted from Carolyn to watch Callie thumb through pages, a text ping from her phone grabbed her attention.

"Patty's on her way back," Callie said while two-thumbing her a snarky reply, *it's about time.*

"She's dealing with it too, sweetie." Jason commented as he saw the text on her screen.

Callie gave Jason a look of exhaustion. Her message was clear. She needed her sister to help share this burden.

"She's pulling into the parking garage. Let's go for a walk or something. Maybe get a drink somewhere."

Jason gave a brief smile and nod to both suggestions. However, a drink, he feared, would either wipe her out or charge her up. Neither was a good solution for them now.

Callie gave her mother a kiss on the cheek before leaving. Jason held back from any engagement except to help Callie pass by and leave the room. Her face remained resigned as they walked the hall to the elevator. As he took her hand, he felt her grip tighten to accept that he was there for her.

As the elevator opened right when they arrived, Jason and Callie both smiled at their apparent good fortune to not to have to wait. A lively conversation coming from inside became louder as the doors opened and Lizzie, Will and Chase emerged. Callie stopped immediately when she saw her children. Jason did not tune-in to the group being family until he recognized Chase from their fight last fall.

The conversation that was jovial in the metal box stopped abruptly as all three of Callie's family members saw Callie standing in the hallway holding another man's hand. Chase's face immediately sank as he recognized Jason. Callie released her grip to the disappointing looks from her children.

"Of course, you're here," Chase muttered in disgust.

Jason stayed silent as Callie went to hug her children.

"Chase, not here, not now," was all she said to him.

After a short discussion on Carolyn's condition, Callie invited her family, with Chase, to dinner before asking Jason if it was okay. He smiled as the words came out of her mouth trying to think of an excuse to bail on the family reunion without abandoning Callie in the process. Callie knew she would have to explain Jason to Lizzie and Will. She still did not know if Chase had ever disclosed her Columbus Day weekend with him to them.

The two groups separated to their cars after agreeing on a place to meet. It was a restaurant familiar to Callie's family that Jason had a feeling he had visited before when in Williamsburg for soccer. When they pulled into the strip mall, his recollection was confirmed. He remembered the family style bistro to have extraordinary food and an even better selection of beer, wine, and spirits.

"You'll like this place," Callie said as they parked.

"I've been here before," Jason smirked knowing it made Callie wonder when and why?

Callie took his hand for support as they walked through the parking lot. They walked past the Maserati Jason remembered from the beach when Chase jumped him during his goodbye to Callie. Jason let go of Callie's hand when her hand loosened its grip and her family was about to come into view.

"Nice car," Chase quipped to Jason as they approached.

Chase remembered Jason's older, Jeep Wrangler from the weekend. His arrogance had to take a stab at Callie's new, old boyfriend, lover, driving the car he paid for.

"It's nice," Jason replied unable to control the urge to stab back.

"But it's a little much for me..... If you know what I mean."

"Boys, really?" Callie interjected. "Let's just have a nice dinner and relax."

When they entered the restaurant, Jason requested a table under Callie's name as the four of them took off to visit the rest rooms. Jason stayed behind to go later in case their table was called early. Of the four, Chase was the first to return.

"I'm surprised to see you here," he stated. "I didn't think Callie had it in her to parade a new boyfriend in front of her mother so soon. Particularly the one that shit all over her thirty years ago."

Jason smiled at the assault.

"Well, there's a lot of truth to that. I'm surprised to," he answered to calm the tension.

Chase smiled as he studied Jason from head to toe. As time passed slowly, his stare continued while Jason's patience plummeted.

"By the way," Jason started slowly to ensure he had Chase's full attention. "I want to thank you for taking my spot as the family's number one, persona non grata, asshole."

Jason smirked as Chase's expression tightened and his chest puffed. He started to lean toward Jason as Callie and Lizzie returned with Will. Callie's face dropped as she saw the two men squaring off with Chase's chest sticking out.

"What did we miss?" she asked. "Chase, Jason just drove me here. Please... Lighten... up."

Chase withdrew from his aggressive stance as Callie's message sunk in.

"Let's just have dinner," she ordered.

The dinner was as expected with well-prepared food and drinks for everyone. As the alcohol calmed nerves, conversation opened on Jason's southern Virginia schooling and how he met and knew Callie. Both the children were intrigued to meet the ex-fiancé they knew existed. The balance of the story was limited to Callie ending the engagement telling Jason to take a hike. He took the hit for her.

Lizzie found Jason likable even if a threat to her dad. Will was less engaged until Jason talked about his social media marketing company. Some of its work had been scrutinized favorably in a marketing class at William and Mary. Jason was happy to share his stories while trying to tie in the similarity of that work to Chase's political campaign consulting. Irritated by Will's fascination with Jason's company that placed insignificant products in movies and with influencers when his firm got congressmen and senators elected, Chase remained unusually quiet as he stewed until the bill came.

"Let me get this one," Jason said while reaching for the bill.

Chase was ahead of him already concerned about how it would look to his kids if mom's new boyfriend bought them, rather HIM, dinner.

"My family. I pay," Chase said feeling sick that he was buying Jason food and drink.

"Thank you," Jason conceded. "I'll buy next time."

Jason knew the comment would sting. The resulting look from Chase showed that it landed with full force. Callie watched the subliminal fight that seemed to be flying over her kids heads and shuffled her chair to indicate she was ready to leave. But the check still had to be processed with tip before they could go.

"Do you have any kids?" Lizzie asked Jason.

"I do," he answered, "four daughters. Unfortunately, they're all older than you."

Callie's eyes lit for a moment then faded to the age distinction.

"Well, Maya is your age," Callie added to Chase's disdain. "She's a rising junior at NC State studying... business?"

Callie looked to Jason for confirmation recalling competitive interests between education and business. Jason's response was a slight eye-roll and shaking of his head.

"I'm studying education at JMU," Lizzie responded.

"I can see it," Jason replied. "You'll make a terrific teacher."

"You don't even know her, and you tell her she'll be great," Chase grumbled jealous that his daughter was so engaged his wife's new boyfriend.

Jason winked at Lizzie. She smiled in appreciation of his comment. She was Callie.

"There is one thing we need to discuss," Chase added. "Where is everyone staying tonight?"

Callie was surprised by the question in front of her children and looked to Jason for support. His suitcase was still in their bedroom at Carolyn's. To claim he was staying anywhere else would easily be uncovered as a lie.

"I was staying at Carolyn's. But I can find a hotel for tonight. My kids are bringing my Jeep tomorrow. I'll probably head back to deal with things at home."

"Home, right," Chase laughed. "Whose home is a dumpy little cottage on the Outer Banks?"

"You live on the beach?... at the Outer Banks!?" Lizzie exclaimed

Her questions were full of excitement until it sank in. She then gave a panicked look to her mother before turning back to Jason.

"You were the Facebook friend at the beach last fall?" Lizzie asked in disbelief before looking at Callie. "I thought you were visiting your girlfriend from home.... Stephanie?"

"Yeah, they're divorced," Chase added as he swirled ice in his glass. "Stephanie was never there."

"Stop it, Chase!" Callie declared before calming her voice for Lizzie. "Lizzie, I was with Jason. We were in separate rooms."

"Still sticking to that story, are ya?" Chase added as his eyes moved from his glass to Callie.

"Don't," she replied. "With everything going on, just don't."

Callie looked to Lizzie then to Will as both sat silently waiting for answers. Lizzie's expression showed hurt. Will was angry as Chase continued to enjoy the jabs he was delivering to make her look like a cheater with the man the kids seemed to like.

"I'll tell you the entire story about who Jason is, and how I ended up visiting him last fall, while your dad golfed with his college buddies, when we can be together, ALONE."

Callie threw the golf clarification to give Chase his due blame for inflaming their already delicate marriage situation.

"I promise. It was all innocent. We are old friends. You both have really good friends of the opposite sex too. That's what this was then."

"And now?" Lizzie asked scanning all the faces at the table.

"I don't know," Callie answered honestly. "And with your grandmother's situation, I'm not going to think about it."

Lizzie looked to Jason for anything he wanted to add. Jason studied her face imagining her as one of his girls. He knew the look from his divorce. He also knew this conversation was best handled in a private setting between family members.

"Lizzie, your mom will tell you everything. What I think doesn't matter."

Callie showed fear as she listened to his reply. As Chase signed the check then closed the small credit card portfolio, they all stood to leave.

"We still have to finalize accommodations," Chase added.

Callie's first thought was to tell him to *Go to hell!* But her better judgment to stay quiet prevailed.

"You all stay at Carolyn's. I'll find a place to stay tonight." Jason said as if final.

"Wrong. You can sleep in Maggie's room again tonight. She's coming in tomorrow. Chase, you can bunk with the kids in the basement. It's done!"

Chase accepted Callie's plan without objection. He was back in the house where he wanted to be. Jason was his primary concern. That asshole was not going to sleep with his wife if he had anything to say about it.

17

Carolyn was awake when Callie brought Will and Lizzie in to visit. Although prepared on what to expect with very specific detail from their mom, Lizzie melted into tears when she saw Carolyn smile then try to speak. What she saw in front of her was her grandmother evaporating away. Will managed to remain poised as he greeted, kissed, and spoke with his grandmother. The sight of all three together depleted the strength Callie had left for the day. She needed some wine to relax.

As the three left Carolyn for the night, they gathered with Jason and Chase in the waiting room. Both were sitting in neutral corners as Callie asked Jason to do on the drive over. His original plan was to drop her then leave for a while. That plan changed with her request to stay nearer to her than Chase could ever be.

The Range Rover and Maserati pulled into the governor's driveway together. The house lights were on which was unusual since Patty stayed at the hospital. The group walked in together to investigate.

"Hello!?" Callie yelled out into front hall.

"Callie!?" a familiar voice rang back from the kitchen.

Relief set in as the intruder they suspected appeared.

"You're supposed to here tomorrow," Callie said as she hugged her sister Maggie.

"I got an earlier flight," she answered as she looked over the group to include Chase and Jason.

"Well, this is a surprise," she said with a look of complete disbelief. "Hi Jason."

Jason felt his chest tighten as the focus of Callie's family and husband rolled from Maggie to him. He laughed at the awkwardness of the situation with Chase in the room. He took a step forward wondering if he should hug her.

"Hi Maggie. I'm sorry to be meeting again under these circumstances."

Maggie watched and enjoyed his squirming before deciding to give him a break with a hug. As she wrapped her arms around him, Jason felt the familiar pain in his neck that Callie would inflict that he used to hate but now coveted. Maggie stepped back as she scanned the group.

"Chase," she added with a mean scent that proved Jason's congratulations to Chase was warranted.

Chase replied with a courteous grumble before leaving with the kids to go down to the dungeon to choose their beds. As they disappeared into the kitchen and could be heard walking down the stairs, Maggie broke out in laughter. Her sister's apparent joy with Chase's discomfort brought laughter to Callie. Jason hesitated then surrendered with only a smile.

"Oh my God. Can this day get any worse?" Callie added. "I need a drink."

As the three started to the kitchen, the front door opened adding Patty, her husband Brian, and their two boys to the mix. Like it or not, Chase was going to have to share his bunk room.

# # # #

The house was full of people but seemed empty. Everyone was scattered doing different things to stay busy. Chase and Will were playing pool as Lizzie Facetimed her friends back home. Maggie was upstairs in her room unpacking as Patty, Brian and their two teenage boys settled in Patty's room and in the basement. The lie that Jason was staying in Maggie's room was blown until Maggie agreed she would say she was sleeping with Callie to give Jason her room. The only people that believed her were the younger kids.

Callie felt completely spent and excused herself to bed around 10:30PM. It was a good optic that she went up before Jason so anything Chase would say would sound jealous, even if right. As she walked out of Jason's sight, Callie detoured to the basement to deal with one lingering issue.

"I need to talk to you," she said after waiting for his pool cue to start toward the cue ball.

The surprise of Callie's voice disrupted his focus. The resulting shank of the shot pocketed both the cue ball and the eight ball together. His game was over.

Chase held a pause as he absorbed within him his frustration for Callie's rude and intentional interruption of his shot. As he turned to look at her, he found his wife with her arms crossed staring back at him.

"Outside," she ordered as she led the way across the basement to the door that lead up to the back patio and garden.

"What the fuck are you doing here?" she whispered angrily.

The light from the sunroom drifted down from above. From her days with young kids running amuck through the yard, she knew that Jason could not see them. However, she was concerned that loud voices would permeate the glass and be heard.

"I brought the kids to be with you," he answered exaggerating the innocence of his intent.

"You're not welcome here anymore. You know that!"

"Yeah, well throw their dad out after he got them here for you. How would that look?"

Chase's strategy was working to get the leverage he needed to stay. Jason Cartwright was not going to be the family's male savior during this crisis.

"Did you bring your slut, whore with you too?" Callie asked. "Have her parked in a hotel for a quickie when I'm at the hospital?"

The stab hit hard leaving Chase in the very unusual position of not having a prepackaged reply.

"Yes, I know about her," Callie finished. "For God's sake, why would you take her with you on your first vacation with the kids without me?"

Fuck, he thought to himself as he waited for Callie to finish. The fact that she knew his last indiscretion was in Nantucket undermined his entire white knight appearance.

"She followed us there. She stayed at a B and B in town," Chase confessed in a *mea culpa* tone.

Callie expression of anger deepened as Chase waited for her to absorb that he did not either invite or take her with them.

"Did you sleep with her Chase?" she asked. "Did you fuck her?"

The graphic insinuation Callie made declared the raw anger she was feeling. Chase knew Callie had been told about his early morning arrivals back at the cottage. Likely by Lizzie.

"Callie, you and I are not together...."

Callie rolled her eyes to his confirmation and lack of discretion with her children.

"Why?" he continued. "Are you fucking him!?"

Callie stood quietly as the pressure built within her to slug the smug look off his face.

"Not yet," she answered. "Not in twenty-eight years."

The finish was a raw nerve for Chase she knew would hurt. It confirmed nothing happened during the October weekend. It also confirmed that she was still faithful to him and their marriage despite his numerous affairs. Most of all, it reminded him that Jason was her first love, her first fiancée, and the one man he feared could show up at any time and take her away.

"What do you think our kids, LIZZIE, thinks of all of this when she knows you were out banging your slut, whore girlfriend all night?"

Chase stood quiet as he looked through the glass at his kids in the game room. For the first time he felt ashamed about his activities outside of their marriage. As he thought about Callie's words, he decided that the best way to fix things, particularly with Lizzie, was to let them go to be either forgotten or forgiven. Happy with that revelation, he returned to real-time to find Callie gone.

# # # #

Callie darted through the basement game room without either a look or comment to anyone. From experience, both Lizzie and Will knew it was best to let her go. They looked at each other knowing that their dad just got his head handed to him on a platter.

As Callie stormed up the basement stairs, she stopped short of the door to collect herself and to make a quiet entrance and walk through of the kitchen up to bed. From the kitchen, she could hear that Jason and Maggie were still in the sunroom where she left them. He was enjoying a bourbon. Maggie had a glass of her mom's Rose' which was a special find last fall that she kept buying.

"Feels strange to be here, doesn't it?" Maggie asked.

Jason took a sip of bourbon and pondered the question. He smiled as he visualized Callie's parents in the room and what they would say. As they faded, an empty sadness filled him as he looked to a Maggie who was considerably older than he remembered.

"I bet this was your dad's favorite room in the house," he answered. "The glass, the view, the top of the hill, the look out over his kingdom."

Maggie smiled as she placed Jason's words to her dad's nature. They affectionately called him *"Big Guy"* because he was. He was larger than life to his daughters and to Jason.

"I think he'd be OK with you being here," Maggie added.

"I hope so. I had a wonderful reconnection with your mom today. She's so loving."

Maggie held her smile as she thought back to comments Carolyn made about Jason and Callie when they were together and after their engagement ended.

"Yes, well, that 'love' depends upon what you're doing at the time, or have done."

Maggie was joking. Everything Carolyn did had the full force of unconditional love behind it. The interactions may have been tense and nasty. But her intent was always pure and loving.

"I'm sorry you missed the last thirty years," Maggie added honestly. "But I'm sure you had your own adventure."

"Well, that's a very long story. But I did end up with four terrific daughters who should all be at the beach together right now."

Maggie blurted a laugh at Jason's female head count.

"Four daughters?" she added. "Did Callie ever tell you our parental decay theory?"

Jason nodded his head and thought about how many times he repeated that theory.

"The forest. I've heard it," he replied.

"First child chops the trees. The SECOND, me, paves the lot," Maggie added the emphasis and a toast to salute herself, "Then the third gets to drive all over it."

"With four," Jason clarified, "the first cuts the trees. The SEC-

OND pulls the stumps. The THIRD paves the lot. And, the fourth drives all over it."

Maggie loved the expanded version and toasted her glass to it. As he responded, she noticed a sadness appear.

"What's wrong?"

"Nothing," he answered. "I've got four wonderful kids. Yet I have this painful regret for the loss of the life I would have had with Callie. It's so strange. I love and would die for any of my girls. But, there's just such... REGRET."

Jason's emphasis on regret intrigued Maggie. She never felt Callie experienced the same sense of loss. Up until the fall Lizzie left for college, Callie always seemed to busy and happy.

"I think," Maggie paused to position the right words, "that it really sucks that we're supposed to choose our mates for LIFE at a time in life when next to nobody is emotionally mature enough to do it all while the hormones to hump everything are raging."

Jason held his laughter thinking through if that was the right thing to do. Maggie was the family's honest talker. She was that way in her twenties; and she continued to be in her fifties. She married a man from California and moved there to be with him. She was an outspoken California liberal as was her husband and two kids that rarely flew east. Jason toasted his glass to Maggie after he realized that she had just released him from his past misdeeds.

"With that, I'm going to say good night," he announced while standing.

"Good night, Jason. I'm glad you're here for her.... particularly with cheater-man downstairs. How messed-up is it that he's here?"

Jason smiled at the thought then nodded. He then headed out with a renewed vigor to go find Callie. He knew the woman he always considered his *ONE* was likely asleep and waiting for him to join her. Her mother and sisters all openly accepted him back into their fold without hesitation. Her kids seemed OK with him being with their mom. All while Chase was under the same roof watching it all unfold.

Callie was curled in a fetal position when he slid in behind her. As he shaped his body to hers, she felt his warmth and presence then reached for his arm to pull him close.

18

The morning started early as Patty, Callie and Jason all appeared at the top of the stairs together. Maggie was still on west coast time and was expected to sleep for a few more hours. The kids and Chase were not going to rise before 9AM. Callie pondered that she never thought about where Chase had settled to sleep until now. She squeezed Jason's hand for comfort while giving him a reassuring smile.

"We have to plan today," she said. "We all just can't arrive at the hospital together."

The two sisters knew there was going to be a few hours of peace before heads started appearing from above and below. The plan they created was to have a rotation of visits with advance checks by who was to arrive on Carolyn's condition to ensure she was strong enough for visitors. Callie and Patty started speculating on care for after she was released from the hospital. The more they talked, the more nervous they got.

"I'm just going to have to move here," Callie said stating the obvious solution.

"Callie, this all can't drop on you," Patty answered.

"You have a job and life in D.C. Maggie's life is in L.A. I am the only one with nothing to keep me anywhere."

As she said the words, she realized Jason was standing next to her.

"Present company excluded, of course," she added quickly with a touch to his hand.

"No offense taken'" he smiled.

The reality of the situation Callie and her sisters were facing was all too familiar. The time, money and emotional demands were going to be exhausting. Jason knew Callie would dedicate everything to provide the best care and support for her mother. He feared that effort would affect her greatly and likely kill them as a couple.

"I think it's great to start shaping plans," he added "But you have time and need more information. Things are going to constantly change. I suggest trying to coral the doctors for real answers and expectations."

His words sounded good. But the situation was still frightening the two sisters as they remained quiet and took another taste of coffee.

# # # #

The sun over the ocean was masked by a cloud cover that was forecasted to last until late afternoon. This eclipse gave Jason's girls opportunity to get the Jeep to Williamsburg and be back in time for the softer afternoon beach sun and happy hour. As they finished their coffee, Rachel declared their *Get Dad His Jeep* mission a *GO* then assigned Maya and Elyse to the Mini Cooper convertible and Faith with her to Jason's Wrangler. The romance of a topless drive in both vehicles up to Williamsburg improved with the lack of sun not being there to fry them. Elyse, who had just arrived from Philadelphia the night before, agreed to go, but only if she did not have to drive.

The girls were on the road by 8AM. A stop at the coffee shop where Callie and Jason first talked after twenty-seven years, was needed for fresh blends and breakfast sandwiches. The pit-stop set them back twenty minutes and Jason about twenty-five dollars.

Enroute now. ETA 10:30.

Please send meeting address.

Jason was surprised by both the text and their estimated time of arrival.

OK. TBD on meeting location. Keep me informed on where you are.

A thumbs-up emoji from Rachel confirmed the loose plan. The girls were on their way with their sunglasses on and music lists playing.

# # # #

The morning lingered as heads kept emerging from downstairs. Maggie finally made her appearance with a notable case of cocktail flu. She slowly meandered to the coffee only to be disappointed by an empty carafe. Unwilling to wait, she found Carolyn's stash of Starbucks pods and made a quick mug of coffee in the Keurig.

The initial plan was for Patty and Callie to visit Carolyn then report back to the house. If Carolyn was up for more visitors, Patty's husband Brian and their two boys would visit followed by Will and Lizzie again. Maggie had an open door whenever she was able to be there.

Chase appeared undaunted as he tried to meld into the family again as if nothing had happened. Jason watched as he walked to position himself around the room for unavoidable conversation. He was working the room like a political hack seeking endorsements. But, only the kids would talk to him.

As the plans were finalized, Chase offered no reaction to being left out. He was happy not to hear Jason's name included which kept them on even footing.

Jason was starting to get concerned as the girl's original ETA came and went without follow-up. He texted their group chat to see where they were. With no final meeting point given, he expected to hear from them.

Got delayed by coffee. Were 20 minutes away from Williamsburg. Whats the address.

Jason looked at the text noting some key deficiencies in punctuation. After asking Callie permission, he texted Carolyn's address to them. He knew the hand-off of the Jeep would be fast; and that they would be on their way back to the beach quickly to enjoy their time in the sun, salt, and sand.

Patty and Callie's departure became delayed when Maggie insisted they go together before disappearing again to get dressed. The lost time made Callie impatient who wanted to be in the room when the doctors made follow-up round to give updates. Jason followed her as she walked out the front door to sit on the stoop. She knew Maggie was going to take a while.

As he sat next to her on the three steps near the front door, he bumped her with his shoulder. The nudge was to bring her back and to let her know he was still there. Her eyes were closed as a smile appeared on her face.

"It's going to be OK," he said to reassure her.

As Callie opened her eyes, she looked back over her shoulder not surprised to find Chase glaring at them over his coffee mug. After a few seconds of return fire, Chase acquiesced then quickly turned and left. Callie felt no guilt for being comforted by Jason. He was there for her instead of chasing other women.

"I could feel it," she said as she turned back to face the front yard. "He's watching us."

Before Jason could turn to look and intervene, loud pop music began bellowing in from the street as his Jeep Wrangler, Maya's Mini Cooper, and his four daughters drove up the driveway. Their mood was elated. They were happy from both the trip together and to see their dad stating they had arrived.

As the cars came to a stop, the motors and music went silent as

181

both sets of girls settled from laughter to a smug stillness.

"We're heeeere," Rachel said loudly not knowing the situation at the house.

A quick shake of Jason's head conveyed the message to shut down the revelry. The faces that were smiling all went blank as they began to get out to say *hello.*

"Do you think you four could've made any louder of an entrance?" Jason asked, annoyed with their behavior.

Callie put her hand on his arm to calm him down.

"It's fine," she said. "Welcome you guys, does anyone need to use the bathroom?"

After four *me's* erupted simultaneously, Callie pointed them the first-floor powder room and gave directions to her bedroom upstairs. The four split into the pairs they drove in as then disappeared to find relief.

The commotion created by the four girls arriving attracted attention while stirring interest in Lizzie and Will to check out their counterparts in Jason's family. Will showed immediate appreciation for Jason's Wrangler with its warn patina, full roll cage, and three inch lift with oversized tires. Lizzie loved Maya's NC State Wolfpack red Mini Cooper convertible with its two white racing stripes down its bonnet.

Chase watched the envy of his kids erupt over two vehicles whose value would barely cover the sales tax on his Maserati. Jason's style and influence over his family was getting alarmingly seductive.

"Hey dad!" Lizzie shouted as she studied Maya's car while not looking at him. "This would be nice to have at school."

"This Jeep is pretty sick too."

Will's infatuation with the Jeep that replaced his drooling over the Maserati upset Chase. There was no correlation in his head that a twenty-year-old male would want a typical twenty-year-old male's type vehicle.

"I'll see what I can do," Chase replied not wanting to either say *yes* or *no* to the statements.

It was a standard political reply he instructed his clients to give on issues that they had no interest supporting. Because of a sketchy driving record, Chase did not have a car while in college. It was a family tradition he continued that his kids felt was dated. Chase knew to agree would affirm Jason to his kids. To say *no* would make him look like a jerk. Taking the politically astute path of neither promising nor dismissing anything was going to push the conversation off until it was forgotten. Just like in politics.

Jason listened from the front hall as their conversations unfolded. He felt a twinge of guilt for making Chase uncomfortable blend with satisfaction for making Chase uncomfortable. Zapping Chase through both Lizzie and Will was a double win.

Callie waited to greet each Cartwright daughter as they reappeared in the front hall. Jason enjoyed watching Rachel, Faith and Maya not hesitate to give her a hug. Elyse, at first, balked. But she followed through to hug the woman in the picture she was meeting for the first time.

After their *hellos*, Callie proceeded to introduce Jason's girls to Patty, her husband Brian and to Maggie, who appeared toward the end. Chase was introduced as "Chase" with no qualifier. The girls were then introduced to Will and Lizzie resulting in a collective banter of *"heys"*. Patty's younger boys were nowhere to be seen.

After the introductions ended, the families migrated to their own space in the front hall to work their plans. The space was tight. But everyone managed to find a spot where they could listen. Elyse noticed and started getting uncomfortable that Will stood almost shoulder-to-should with her while facing in a different direction.

After a few seconds, the crowds started to move. The Cartwright girls were thanked for their successful delivery of the Wrangler, given permission to get lunch, and released to head back to the beach. As they turned to look for Callie to say goodbye, Elyse ran into Will who was still standing next to her even though his family had dispersed.

"I'm sorry," she said as he stepped to maintain his balance.

"No problem," he answered before extending his hand. "Will."

Elyse shook Will's hand as she looked at Rachel who was dying of laughter behind him. Embarrassed, a red wash appeared on Elyse's cheeks as she had to deal with the younger, preppie, frat boy trying to introduce himself.

"Elyse," she answered.

"Where do you go to school?" he asked.

"I don't," she replied smugly. "I've graduated and live in Philly."

Rachel gave Jason a look to suggest intervening. To keep the peace, he shook his head *no* to let it play out. The preppy, William and Mary, frat boy was going to be schooled by a Temple Owl's sarcastic Philadelphia blow-off. Elyse had Jason's sarcasm. He cringed to think about what was likely coming.

"So, are you hanging around here?"

Elyse looked again to Rachel as the three sisters were now standing together watching and listening to the pitch.

"I guess. I'm heading back to the beach for a few days with my sisters," Elyse answered. "Then I'm going back to Philadelphia, my job, and... to my wife."

Jason's eye closed as he shook his head in complete disbelief as each sister spun away holding their mouths not to be heard laughing. Will smiled as the message was received that he had *no shot*. Callie felt relief with her amusement while shaking her head feeling sorry that her son's efforts she did not want to succeed sank. Chase could only give his son an *E* for effort.

"That's cool," Will answered trying to remain charming. "Well, I'll be here if you want to play. Or, I can drive to the beach if that's easier. I go to William and Mary. We go to the beach all the time."

Elyse was finding it hard to not laugh. He was trying. And to her that was worth some credit. Her sisters were beginning to lose interest and wanted to get going. Callie and Jason looked at each other, smiled and decided that there was nothing to worry about.

"I'm good Will. But, if I get an itch, I'll call ya."

"That'd be fun," he replied trying to appear cool while feeling the sting of rejection.

Elyse rejoined her sisters as they said goodbye to Callie and their dad. Jason walked them to the Mini for their send-off. As they backed to a point where they could turn around, Lizzie peered through the window envious of the four sisters, the car, and the two-hour ride they had together back to the beach. Although they looked like a circus car with no top, she wanted to go with them.

Will watched through the front door as they drove away and disappeared. As he looked back into the room, he glanced at his dad with an expression Chase had never seen before. Patty and Maggie were ready to roll as he walked past his mom as she filled her travel mug with coffee.

"Will?" she asked, "What was that all about?"

"Nothing mom," he answered with a disturbing glean. "I just figured if her dad is doing you then, well, you know."

Callie's fury erupted resulting in an action she never thought she would do. The smug look of disrespect and defiance on her son's face had to be removed. The smack of her open hand across his cheek was as loud as the tree limb breaking at Fox Farm. The horror of his statement and her involuntary reaction devastated her.

"Callie!" Chase yelled seeing his son standing bent over.

Callie was shaking as she watched her son fighting the pain she just inflicted. Her eyes continued to show a bright red of anger as she continued to face him. As Will limped away in silence, Callie began to cool to realize the magnitude of what she had just done. As she scanned the room looking for Chase, she found him standing frozen in the doorway to the front hall.

"You! You FUCKING, son of a bitch! You're the cause of all of this!"

Chase stood still as she spoke. Patty and Maggie watched Will slink past him as Chase ran options on what to do.

"We need to get out of here," Chase said before looking to Jason. "Move your fucking Jeep.... Please."

Chase's tone was serious and angry, but calm. Jason empathized that Chase was in a no-win situation. The best thing to do was to separate, cool down, then rebuild. Jason felt partly responsible for Will's actions as he walked out ahead them to give Chase his exit path to a safe spot with his son. The distinct roar of the Maserati starting confirmed that the two were leaving.

As the car left the driveway, Jason returned to the front door to find Callie, Patty and Maggie on their way out. Callie was struggling to hold together bravely. But it was clear, her state of mind was emotionally shot.

"Cal," he said reaching out to her.

Callie walked by him without a look. A fast raise of her arm to deflect his sent the message that she had to go to cope with everything. In less than a minute, Chase, Will, Patty, Maggie and Callie were gone.

19

The drive back to the beach cottage was uneventful. The sun continued to hang behind the layer of clouds to keep its blistering heat at bay. The collective playlist they made the night before included mutual favorites that at least three out of four enjoyed at any given time. The cottage was producing what Jason wanted. It was a spot where his girls would visit, enjoy each other, and hopefully spend some time with him.

As they finished their drive, Maya was excited with the thought of not having to put the car's top up right away. The Wrangler was gone leaving the best parking under the house open for her Mini. Jason was adamant to the point of annoyance about her closing the top each night because of the salt mist corrosion on electronics and fabrics that could happen. Maya knew they had at least one run left to the store before day's end. She was ready to hit the sand and would put the top up then.

As the Mini slowed to make the turn into the driveway, the girls saw Jason's Volvo Cross Country parked in the Wrangler's spot in the shade.

"That's weird," Rachel commented.

Maya parked behind the Volvo in the sun next to Elyse's car. As they walked past, each touched Jason's Volvo to confirm it was there, looked inside for things distinctly their dad, then headed up to the house to look for more clues as to why it was there.

As Rachel reached the top of the stairs, she noticed a woman with shoulder length brown hair sitting on the bench that overlooked the water. Rachel's first thought was to wonder why and how Callie beat them there. But the Volvo not being with Jason was why the Jeep had to be delivered to Williamsburg. The woman on the bench was not Callie.

The sister chatter that followed Rachel worked its way down the walkway to attract the attention of Jason's brown, fuzzy companion who stirred to attention and darted to greet them.

"Zoeeee!" they shrieked in unison as she stopped at their feet to be smothered by pats of love.

The woman waiting on the bench heard the commotion and turned to look to see what drew Zoe's attention. Her hope was to see Jason. Her anxiety spiked when she saw his four daughters instead. Clara fixed her hair then put on a baseball cap as the four girls approached her.

"Hi," Rachel stated amused to be meeting a second pretty, appropriately aged, mystery woman who happened to be driving her dad's car with his dog.

"Hi girls, my name is Clara. I'm returning your dad's car and Zoe from Fox Farm," she answered.

It all started to come together for the girls why the Volvo and Zoe were brought to the house by someone they did not know. But the woman, who was very pretty, fit, just their dad's type, and eerily similar to Callie, confused them. They knew he left Asheville in a hurry with Callie to get her to Williamsburg. Leaving the car was necessary. Leaving his dog elevated the intrigue to a much higher level.

"First, introductions," Rachel said.

"Let me guess," Clara asked to interject a spirit of fun.

Clara rattled off each name without hesitation identifying each girl correctly. The speed and accuracy of Clara's rollcall was impressive to each of them. Their desire to find out who she was to their dad grew bigger with each correct name.

"Have you been here long?" Rachel asked.

"About thirty minutes."

"Do you need to use the bathroom?" Maya queried thinking about the drive from Asheville plus thirty minutes.

"No, I stopped at an awesome coffee shop on the strip," Clara answered. "If you haven't been, I…"

"Oh. We've been," they answered together.

"It was hard to leave those pastries. We could use a place like that near the cabins."

"Speaking of which," Maya pondered, "How are you getting back?"

Clara paused as she looked at each of them wait for her answer.

"I don't know?" she admitted almost giddy with the thought. "This trip was impulsive which is totally not me."

Clara giggled nervously at the blank faces that were listening. She knew there had to be an airport nearby. If not, then she could take a bus. But that would take forever. Jason would help her get back. She left the farm in able, but not *really able*, hands. Anxiety started to build again as her conversations started bottlenecking; and he was not there to solve her problem. Given the urgency that made him leave the farm, calling him to plan Zoe's and the Volvo's return so quickly when there was no real need seemed rude.

The girls began to feel sorry for the lovely, Asheville woman who had made the nice gesture and long drive not to be able to personally deliver the car and his best friend to Jason. They invited Clara in for some refreshment and to help plan her return trip. As they walked in, Maya texted Jason

> *Clara brought the volvo and Zoe home. She needs*
> *to get back to Ashville. Suggestions?*

# # # #

What next? was Jason's first thought when he opened Maya's text. The thought came to him even before feeling any comfort in knowing that the four girls in Maya's ridiculously small convertible made it safely back to the cottage.

After Callie's earlier departure, there were no attempts by her to reach Jason by either text or phone. Chase and Will remained at-large while Lizzie disappeared to the basement game room. Brian and his two boys decided to hike to the James River to stay busy until Patty called with instructions.

Clara's unexpected arrival at the beach made no sense. The farm had adequate staff to operate for days without her. But there was no need for her to drive the seven hours to the cottage unless something was wrong. Jason's first thought was that Zoe was sick.

The face of Clara's phone illuminated through her shorts pocket as it vibrated. She was sitting next to Elyse on a stool at the kitchen island. Elyse had her lap top open to view travel options back to Asheville as the rest of the girls settled in looking for the lunch they put off on the way home.

The best option for time and price was a one-way car rental back Asheville. The clock on her phone showed 1PM when she went to answer the call that was coming. Seeing Jason's name on her iPhone's screen made her nervous. She was also thankful she had silenced her phone to silence his dedicated ring tone of Led Zeppelin's *Stairway to Heaven*.

"It's your dad," she said to Elyse as she answered. "Hey, how are things with Callie's mom?"

The casual answer surprised Jason. Clara typically answered in a more serious tone.

"So, I hear you've met the girls," he said smiling knowing she was looking at all four of them wondering who and when they narc'd.

"Jason."

"Got a few with you now?" he asked.

"Elyse is helping me to rent a car back to Asheville," Clara answered. "Permission to put it on the company card.... sir."

Elyse rolled her eyes from her laptop to Clara then back. A smile came to her face with the flirtation she just heard. *Good luck lady,* she thought recalling Callie and the Williamsburg house that hosted the car swap earlier. The remaining conversation focused on Zoe, who was just anxious to have been left but happy to be back at the beach, that the car drove well, and that Ruth, Clara's right hand at the farm, was left in charge. To Elyse, all seemed acceptable to her dad. Clara closed with an overstated compliment about Jason's oceanfront cottage before saying goodbye. The pause and look on her face as she signed off both amused and concerned Elyse. As Clara rejoiced in her successful call with her boss, Elyse began to put together the pieces of the conversation she heard.

"This place is fantastic," Clara declared as she surveyed the interior of the cottage.

"Why don't you stay and enjoy this," Elyse offered for reasons beyond just being nice. "The rental agency closes at four. It's 1PM now. You'd still get home before midnight."

Clara did some quick math in her head to realize she would miss the dinner deliveries even if she left immediately. Her 6AM departure was also catching up with her. She had an overnight bag with a swimsuit in case Jason insisted that she stay. But that was all predicated on JASON being there, not his four, adult daughters.

"I'd love to if it's not too much of a bother," she replied still anxious about who was there, and who was not.

"It's no problem," Elyse insisted. "Callie stayed here the night she went to see my dad at your place. Faith washed the sheets on my dad's bed. So, you're welcome to stay overnight if you want."

As the pressure of panic set in on Clara, the three remaining sisters re-emerged in bikinis to head out to the beach.

"We've decided that you'll make lunch," Maya said to Elyse who was annoyed with being behind in getting changed.

"I'll help you," Clara smiled.

"Clara's going to join us for lunch, some beach time, and maybe overnight," Elyse added to bring everyone up to date.

Faith, Rachel, and Maya raised then dropped their chins in unison happily acknowledging Elyse's message.

"Excellent," Faith added. "This should be fun."

As Clara wandered into the kitchen to survey the refrigerator, each sister shared looks to show a mutual interest in uncovering who and how Clara fit in the picture. Their dad's series of trips to Asheville had a reason. Clara's arrival seemed oddly timed with Callie's.

As Elyse walked back to change, she passed Rachel on her way back to the living room.

"Get this," Elyse whispered. "She works for dad and that Fox Farm thing. I think he bought it."

Rachel responded with a muffled, light laugh. Everything was beginning to make sense.

"This is going to be fun"

# # # #

With no word from Callie, Jason began scrolling his phone for something to do in Williamsburg. The hike to the river that Brian and the two boys embarked on, that seemed boring then, was now looking like a lost opportunity for fun. The silence in the house, compounded with the lack of the unappealing options beyond Historic Williamsburg, were making him antsy to move. To kill his boredom, he decided to go for a drive. When Callie needed him, she would either text or call; and, he would be moving.

Jason's first stop was a second drive back through William and Mary that brought back fun memories of his tours with Rachel and Elyse. Faith attended a week-long soccer camp there hoping to win the attention of the coach. He smiled while remembering getting lost as they took the scenic route home through central Virginia. A detour that added two hours to their trip.

As time passed, Jason began to worry about Callie and Carolyn. No word meant that nothing, either good or bad, likely happened. But Callie's disposition when she left the house, without even a look, worried him. The GPS showed that the hospital was a few miles away. Jason decided to stop instead of call. If everything was fine, she'd send him off again. If things were not going well, he would be there for her.

# # # #

The corridor to Carolyn's hospital room remained littered with the same computer carts, gurney beds and meal wagons he remembered from the day before. His initial thought leaving the elevator was *what a shitty place to die*. Patients in gowns, along with guests, doctors, nurses, aids, and therapists all meandered through the narrow hallway in a controlled chaos. The sight reminded him of his parent's numerous stays in hospitals. The only good memory of those stays were the discharges.

As Jason turned the corner, he saw Chase standing in the hall next to Will. They were conversing with someone through the doorway to Carolyn's room. The mood seemed calm. He slowed to a stop as he drifted to the wall to watch.

The conversation he saw looked friendly. Chase smiled at a comment then returned some words Jason could not hear. Will stood anxiously next to his dad rocking from foot to foot as if both nervous and happy he got away with something really bad. As the conversation seemed to end, Callie emerged from the doorway to hug Chase holding on affectionately for a few seconds. She then turned to Will to give him the same hug and hold. As her eyes opened over Will's shoulder, she saw Jason down the hall standing still watching the scene in front of him finish. Her eyes held to his as she stepped back. Chase and Will looked to see what caught her attention.

There was nothing Jason could do now that all three of them knew he was there. To storm off would insinuate he had been betrayed which he was not sure he could claim regardless of what was just happened. Callie's expression was one of being caught and sorry. He knew she was emotionally fragile which gave reason to excuse just about anything. It was the same excuse they used in the fall when he let her sleep in his bed. He could not be a hypocrite in this situation. But he did want to learn the truth.

Chase excused himself from Callie and Will to make his way toward Jason. There was obvious bad news coming through him that showed on Callie's face. Jason's body tensed as Chase arrived.

"What you've been told about me, our marriage, and my extra-curricular activities are all true. I've admitted that to Callie and did a shitty job in seeking forgiveness. I just want you to know that I've had twenty-five years in this family. And I want my family back. That compares to your ZERO."

Jason's deeper concerns about Callie not calling were proving to be more than he thought. Two, massive, over-the-top moments of Carolyn's stroke and Callie striking Will in a fit of rage had everyone rethinking their positions. *The good of the family* was back in Callie's head.

"So, what I'm saying is GAME ON. I'm going to fight to WIN her back."

Jason exhaled to relieve the pressure building inside of him. Chase's declaration to fight for his wife again was almost a welcome development. Callie's process to separate from Chase was forced by Chase. This competition would require a true assessment of her love for Chase and for him. That was his charge to her in October. That decision had to be made before he knew there could be a *them*.

"That's fine with me," Jason said trying to blow off his challenge. "But I'm not going to fight you for her. I'm just here to love her. If she wants you more than me, I'll disappear. HER HAPPINESS is what matters most."

Chase's look and laugh blew-off Jason's position. He followed with a wave to Will to leave. Callie remained where she was not breaking eye contact with Jason as he waited for Will to pass by. It was time for them to talk.

Callie had found and used a small sitting room at the end of the corridor when she needed time earlier to think. She knew it was a quiet place where they could talk privately. As Jason approached, he glanced into the room to see Carolyn asleep with Maggie and Patty sitting quietly by her side. The collective worry and pain on their faces was obvious. Hope seem to be fading. Callie pointed to move them to privacy.

The sitting room was the same size as Carolyn's hospital room. It hosted two small couches and a few waiting room chairs. An old desk was used to accommodate the complimentary coffee service. A small refrigerator was placed in its footwell. No one was using the room when they entered. Callie closed the door that was usually propped open.

"I..." Callie started.

"Shhhhhh," Jason said as he put his finger to her lips.

The action immediately sent them both back in memory to Callie's last night at the beach cottage. Their second night of innocent cuddling to fall asleep in his bed erupted into kissing, half undressing, and near love making until Jason stopped it. His reason was to preserve her integrity and marriage. She was not a cheater. And, regardless of his feelings and their opportunities, he would never let her reach the point of adultery. When they stopped, Callie shushed his explanation in the same way as she settled into a half-undressed cuddle, skin-to-skin, for the night. Callie never admitted that to either Chase or their marriage counselor.

"Callie, this is too much for you," he said as tears welled in his eyes.

"It's not what you think you saw," she answered.

"You're not there yet for us to happen. You need to close your marriage which will take more time. You also need to be here for your mom which is exponentially more important. As I said last fall, I'll be where you can find me. YOU need to take care of yourself, your mother, your family, and to find your own inner happiness."

Jason's words made sense. But his declaration to be leaving was still painful. Tears appeared in Callie's eyes to provide the needed release of anguish she was feeling. Her mother's health, striking her son, and having her marital failure flare up in front of her family in such an ugly way were swamping her abilities to cope. Jason was right. Pressure had to be released for her to get through all of it. He was the easiest part to let go.

"I'm heading back to the beach," he finished. "Text, call.... COME! for that matter. It's all there for you if you need it. I'm there for you whenever you need me."

Callie smiled as she reached for a hug. The tight pull on his neck created the pain he needed again to feel from her again. Her love was reassuring as it transmitted its warmth from her body to his. She held on until her strength gave out.

Jason asked to say goodbye to Carolyn, Patty and Maggie before leaving. As he and Callie appeared in the door, her sisters could see both had been crying. Jason looked to Carolyn, who was still sleeping peacefully. He still owed her the apology for the cancelled wedding that he never had the courage to give.

As he stepped next to the bed and took her hand, Carolyn gave no return grip as her boney hand remained limp in his. Tears fell from his eyes as studied her face in her quiet, peaceful state. Before leaving, he bent down to give her a kiss on her forehead. It was a gesture Callie's kids did before leaving her room; but, Chase did not when he was given the chance. As he backed away from the bed, Jason gave a quick wave and smile to Patty and Maggie to show his appreciation for the welcome they gave him. He then took Callie's hand as they left together back into the hallway.

"I'll say goodbye here, Cal," Jason said stopping them both outside the door. "Let me know what's going on, and if you need anything."

Callie hugged Jason tightly one last time before giving him a slow, soft kiss. She watched as he backed away then turned to leave. Her eyes stayed on him waiting for a look-back. He turned the corner to the elevators without a glance.

20

It took a while, but Clara decided that she could not visit the ocean without taking a swim. Her bag was packed with a one piece she wore on a trip to the Bahama's with Tom a few years earlier. It still fit, looked current, and was not a *mom* suit. Maya was hot and up for a swim when Clara appeared at the chairs suited and ready to tackle the surf. The two of them entered the water together then were quickly joined by the remaining three sisters.

The water had a refreshing, warm chill. The airiness of the surf that bubbled about was a wonderful contrast to the creek water and, more recent, pond experience. Clara, like Jason, was not called to the beach like the others. She loved the mountains. But an occasional visit to the ocean was always fun.

Each woman entered the water with a boogie board to help fight the waves out, to use as a float, and to ride back in. Jason's ongoing concern about the strong rip currents created his *house rule* that everyone swam with a floatation device. His was a life-saving bullet that he kept in tow during his morning swims. It also proved to be a helpful tool on a number of dire occasions to rescue others from the pull of the surf during his short owner-ship of the cottage.

After a few successful rides on the waves, the five huddled in the water while bobbing up and over the incoming swells. Their conversation was fun and kept light to the girl's schools and jobs. Clara did that intentionally knowing that people, in general, like to talk about themselves. Jason shared that as his favorite tactic to keep conversations going when he did not want to share anything about himself. Rachel and Elyse worked hard to keep from asking direct ownership questions about Fox Farm.

As they emerged from the surf, each woman found a chair to relax. Clara felt both exhilarated and exhausted by the swim and conversation. She also had lost all sense of time during her lunch, swim, and chat. When she checked her phone, she saw 3:45PM show giving her fifteen minutes to get to the car rental agency that was twenty minutes away.

"Problem?" Maya asked smiling after watching Clara's face sink.

"I'm going to miss the car rental," she answered.

Maya looked to Rachel who was also gleaming with excitement.

"Oh, you can push that off until tomorrow," Rachel interjected. "It won't cost you anything. I do it all the time."

"Problem solved then. What's the worst that can happen?" Maya replied in a cavalier tone. "You're welcome to stay."

Clara felt both delight and fear as she was presented with the easy invitation. There was a definite connection to Jason's daughters that she appreciated as a childless woman. She also suspected a conspiracy between the four to get her to lose track of time to keep her there. But the warmth of the setting, the friendliness of the girls, and her opportunity to learn more about Jason was too much to pass up.

"I'm not going to lie," she answered with a smile. "I'd love to stay if I can."

Rachel looked at her sisters to get consensus. It was already decided. But they wanted it to look ceremonial.

"You can. And, you will," she declared.

Clara smiled, happy to now have plans. She texted Ruth at Fox Farm to inform her of her delayed status. Ruth's acknowledgement was confident and immediate. Elimination of that worry enabled Clara to relax in her chair to enjoy the remainder of the afternoon on Jason's beach.

"Happy hour is officially open," Rachel declared as she folded her chair to leave. "It'll be on the bench in ten. Come when you're ready."

Clara stayed seated with remaining three sisters as Rachel stepped away. The three were facing the house to follow the sun as it was in descent over the western sky. Clara stayed facing the water. She could watch the sunset anytime. The roll of the waves was hypnotic and what she wanted to see. Avoiding over-exposure to the sun's harmful rays was also always a goal.

When Rachel reappeared at the bench area overlooking the beach, she shouted while ceremoniously lifting a yellowish pitcher and a pile of red Solo cups. Sunning on the sand was transitioning to sunning in the late afternoon on the deck with refreshments.

When Clara did not respond to the call, Maya checked to find her asleep in her chair. The early start, long drive, and excitement at the beach had wiped her out. Maya tapped her shoulder softly to call her back. As she woke, she was embarrassed to have been sleeping. She immediately wiped her mouth to clear any feared drool. She then smiled to recognize Maya.

"It's happy hour," Maya announced. "We're all going up to the deck."

"That's great," Clara answered still working the sleep affects out of her head and mouth. "I'm going to enjoy this a little bit longer."

"The view's even better up there," Maya encouraged. "But, come up when you're ready."

Clara smiled as Maya folded her chair then walked away. She took a moment to admire the setting. Her gaze moved to survey the complete shoreline north and south. Her thoughts that built with each sight were how nice it was that Jason had captured the best of both worlds in his two properties. And, how lucky he was to have four healthy, beautiful, and gracious daughters.

# # # #

Clara appeared at the top of the stairs as Rachel was finishing her initial pours of Margaritas. Each sister had settled on the three-sided bench wrapped in an oversized beach towel. They had a clean, folded towel waiting for Clara on the bench.

Clara's late arrival to happy hour missed witnessing the chemistry that concocted what she was about to be offered. Rachel's 50:50 blend of Tequila to Margarita mixer was delicious and potent. Clara's cup was poured from the bottom which historically proved to have a higher percentage of tequila than the top. Faith blamed Rachel's poor stirring technique for the result. When she offered to teach her the technique she learned in the Virginia Tech science labs, Rachel declined.

"Welcome Clara," Rachel declared with a lift of her cup. "To the sun, the salt, and the sand. May dad never get tired of it."

The sisters laughed as they all raised their cups in unison to the toast. Clara watched, smiled then awkwardly joined the ritual by lifting her cup to theirs.

"I could get used to this," she said in a quiet voice as she took her first sip.

As the surprisingly heavy load of tequila touched the back of her throat, Clara convulsed forward. She covered her mouth to keep what was in there, in there, before coughing. The girls laughed as she smiled trying to stay with the fun of the moment. Not to be outdone by a bunch of college girls, Clara smiled again as she tipped her glass to the group struggling to ward off more coughing. As her breathing returned to normal, the five settled into the bench to enjoy their drinks and the softer afternoon sun.

"Hey girls!"

The voice was familiar and always seemed timed to the opening of happy hour. Rachel looked to confirm it was Rebecca before inviting her up.

"I saw the Volvo and wanted to check with your dad about our trip to Asheville," Rebecca said as she reached the top of the stairs.

The first face she saw in the group was Clara's sitting on the end of the bench facing the water. At first, Rebecca thought she saw Callie. The two women had physical similarities. And Rebecca expected to see her there with Jason after her earlier visit. But as Clara came in to focus, Rebecca smiled then looked to Maya with an expression of *another one, really?*

Maya's response was to smile then roll her eyes. She then tipped her cup to salute the apparent popularity of her dad. Rebecca was intrigued with the new arrival and decided it would be best if she stayed to chat. Rachel was ahead of her thinking and handed her a cup full of Margarita to start the conversation. After taking her first taste, Rebecca's eyebrows lifted followed by a toast of her cup to compliment the day's blend.

"Rebecca," she said to Clara as she extended her hand.

Clara stood to the greeting and to accept her handshake.

"Clara," she answered, "From Asheville… Fox Farm, that is. Outside of Asheville… in between Lake Lure…. and Asheville."

Faith, Elyse, and Maya all looked at each other and giggled. They knew the coming conversation was going to be good. Like their dad, Rebecca had a way to pull information out of people in conversation. Being a doctor required that.

"Terrific," Rebecca answered. "You can answer all of my questions then. We're sooo excited to be going."

As Rebecca moved to settle her lean, forty-five-year-old body on the bench next to Clara's, Rachel noticed that they we about the same age. Rebecca's strawberry blond to Clara's brown hair plus a few inches in height were their only differences. All four girls listened as Rebecca asked specific Fox Farm questions. Elyse and Rachel had some additional questions of their own they wanted to throw into their conversation, but decided not to. As they chatted, both Clara and Rebecca finished their first Margaritas that Rachel gladly refreshed with a second.

As their third Margarita appeared, Rebecca's phone lit with a call from her family looking for dinner. Clara smiled as Rebecca stood to say goodbye with new excitement to visit Fox Farm in a few weeks. As she moved to make her exit down the stairs, Zoe sprang to attention and sprinted up the walkway towards the house.

All six women noticed Zoe's erratic rise from sleep and run to the cottage. When they turned to see what captured her attention, Jason rose from bending down behind the railing after greeting his dog. Surprised by the audience he had attracted, he gave a quick wave to the women huddled on the bench. The alcohol that was riding easy in Clara until now kicked-in when she saw him.

"Dadeeees here," all four daughters shouted in unison.

Rachel's attention shifted from her dad to watch Clara's reaction. She noted Rebecca watching Clara respond too. As expected, Clara was showing signs of embarrassed giddiness to see Jason.

"Could this get any better?" Rachel whispered through her cup to Rebecca as she watched her dad walk closer.

# # # #

Maya shook her head as the crowd greeted her dad's return with hugs and excitement. With the headcount she had, compared to the three rooms with six total sleeping slots, she knew, she was going to be pushed to a couch. It was the same situation as family holidays when she would be relegated to the kids' table with her younger cousins. Guests were seated first followed by older family. The younger family members got what was left. The only consolation was that she expected Jason to insist that Clara have a room of her own. That meant Faith, as her roommate, was destined to be on a couch with her.

Clara could see by the reception Jason received that his family was tight. A hug followed by a push and a giggle was the common thread through the greetings he received from his oldest down through the youngest. She held back her approach uncertain of the reception she was going to get for impulsively driving the Volvo and Zoe seven hours back to the beach. Particularly, since she had no plans on how to get home.

As Jason separated from his daughters, they returned to the cottage to refill the pitcher and to make room for more. Jason smiled to Rebecca as he approached giving her a hug. He then placed his hand on Clara's shoulder to recognize she was there.

"Looks like you-all have started without me," he said with an anxious stance that showed he was uncomfortable.

"We have," Rebecca smiled, "and you have some catching up to do."

Jason smirked to the comment then looked to Clara. She found his eyes and suspicious expression haunting as he waited to speak.

"Welcome to *Serenity Now*," he said to lighten the conversation.

Clara's face lit with a smile knowing the Seinfeld reference from episodes she watched with her husband Tom. Although never titled, Jason loved the saying and often thought of the cottage as worthy of the it. With everything happening with his life, kids, Callie, and Clara, *Serenity Now* was desperately needed and now on its way out from the cottage in a yellowish pitcher with ice.

Rebecca stayed to talk after declaring left-over night via text to her family. The three shared collective stories of their histories in school, early life, and careers. Rebecca had insights for Clara about Tom's condition that comforted her continued guilt from not having sought help earlier in his fight. Rebecca found Clara fascinating through her optimism and strength as both an entrepreneur and a cancer survivor.

"I've never had cancer," Clara said as she shook off the compliment.

"Sweetie," Rebecca replied in her soothing blend of southern accent and doctor speak. "When a family member has cancer, everyone is afflicted by it. Just because Tom didn't survive does not NOT make you a cancer survivor. You are forging ahead. You're a survivor and deserve the title."

Throughout the start of the conversation, Jason's girls moseyed in and out of the area as interest in the topics and phone driven distractions warranted. At one point, Jason was asked for his wallet that he surrendered without question. When the box of fresh pizza arrived, he immediately offered to pay for it without thinking.

"You already did, dad," Elyse laughed. "We have ours inside. Enjoy."

The intensity of the conversation had reached the point where an hour seemed like minutes. The smell of the pizza, however, grabbed each of them and ignited their appetites. Jason topped off everyone's drink as Rebecca opened the box. Three plastic plates and a zip-lock bag of utensils were included as part of Elyse's delivery.

"I have to be very careful here," Rebecca said as she raised a slice to her mouth. "If I drip any of this sauce on me my kids will go ballistic."

Pizza on the deck was a weekly habit. As he chewed, he visualized Callie next to him on their last night together in October. But at that time, the sun had already set; and the air was much cooler. There was an eerie presence of her there with them.

"Well, look at the time," Rebecca stated as she wiped her mouth with a napkin. "It's time for me to leave *Serenity Now* to return to *Chaos Over There*."

Jason laughed as he shared the humor of his selected name combined with knowing what she was returning to. He toasted his glass as Rebecca took another piece of pizza to go.

"Never one and done," she laughed. "Clara, you have to experience a happy hour next time you're here."

"Sounds great and scary at the same time," Clara answered uncomfortable with the suggestion.

Given what she discussed at the *Flying Dutchman* with Callie, she would never expect an invitation to visit as long as she was still single.

"Oh, it's fun," Rebecca promised. "Just as long as you don't have to drive anywhere after."

Rebecca spun and was down the stairs off onto the sand before Callie could comment. They watched as she continued to walk and struggle to eat the pizza she took. Using an exaggerated lean while taking a bite, it was obvious that Rebecca was determined to not to show her family that she had a better dinner than they did.

"She's funny," Clara observed while still trained on the amazing figure out in the sand.

Jason remained quiet to the comment as he waited for her to reorient back to him. Clara could feel the weight of his look. She paused to look back hoping to find something to say that would make her presence at *Serenity Now,* serene.

"Want to take a walk?" Jason asked to give her more time.

Jason whistled to the house to let them know that the remains of the pizza were there plus the dishes and debris from their dinner. His message was that if they wanted the pizza, then they had to deal with the plates. Faith waved from the table as the four girls stood to watch Jason disappear down the stairs with Clara. They let Zoe go to catch up to them and laughed as her bum and tail waddled down the walkway then out of sight down the stairs.

"Oh, I'd love to be listening to that conversation," Rachel remarked sarcastically.

"No chance," Maya replied. "Too little, too late."

"Care to bet on that?"

"Ten bucks," Maya answered.

Faith looked to Elyse to ask if they should get in on the action.

"You guys in?" Rachel asked the two. "We can build a pot for both. Winner takes all."

Faith laughed thinking back to the short time they shared with Callie and the incomplete history they got. Clara was a new arrival with no history except for their dad's secretive runs to Asheville all spring and summer. Both women were similar in appearance. Clara looked about five years younger. The rest of it was unknown. The scientific process she was applying was short the critical data needed to make a decision.

"I'm in!" Elyse said. "Ten bucks on Clara to win."

A laugh erupted as the three in the wager looked to Faith for her decision.

"There's not enough information!" Faith said positioning to not participate.

The eyes of her sisters remained steadfast. She was going to have to chicken-out to get out of participating.

"Oh OK," Faith answered. "Ten bucks on Callie to balance out the karma."

Maya raised her hand to welcome Faith's confidence and ten dollars to the pot. When they looked back down the waterline for Jason and Clara, they were gone.

# # # #

"You know," Jason said. "You have royally screwed up the sleeping arrangements at the cottage."

Clara's eyes, which were watching each step she took through the wash of the waves, closed. She felt a pressure build because of the truth her surprise visit was sending after their pond frolic and dinner up in the mountains. Jason stayed by her side as she remained quiet. He then shoulder-bumped her looking for a reply.

"I'm sorry if this is awkward for you," she said. "I'm even more sorry for how awkward this is for me."

Jason watched her put her thoughts together. He knew why she was there. The two of them flirted many times before their dinner together and play in the pond. Clara was a woman he would have found attractive at any point in his life. In many ways, she was like Callie in build and personality. They both were his *type* that fit many girls he dated in his earlier years.

"This isn't awkward for me and shouldn't be for you."

"Awkward is a bad choice of words," she answered. "You know if Tom were still alive, I wouldn't have looked at you beyond being a client and an investor…. I loved him that much."

Jason smiled at the sentiment he understood too well. Tom was Clara's *ONE*.

"If Tom were still alive," he answered. "You wouldn't have needed an investor."

Clara acknowledged the correction with a smirk. She recalled her mother saying that when God takes something away, he usually puts something in its place. It may not be immediate and obvious. But it happens. She smiled to the thought as she looked at him for the first time on their walk.

"What?"

"Nothing. Just something my mother said to me came to mind."

"Don't go walking on dark beaches with strange men?"

"No," she laughed. "Although you can be strange… let's say, quirky… at times. But, you're no stranger to me."

Jason smiled to the comment and put his arm around her shoulder. The embrace was unconscious and meant to be supporting. He held her close as he finished his enjoyment of her comment. As he let go, Clara felt him pull away even as he stayed a few inches from her.

The awkward silence that followed was familiar from Jason's time walking with Callie. The air required a delicate balance of politeness and curiosity without presenting anything suggestive.

"I can sleep on the couch," Clara added. "Or get a hotel room."

Jason appreciated the tactical change of the conversation back to his opening. It was something he would have done if he wanted to avoid the conversation he knew they needed to have. But the ongoing relationship they needed to maintain to run Fox Farm required that they address feelings now instead of setting them aside for another time. To not do that would only make things harder later and likely have catastrophic managerial impacts on his latest business investment.

"Ok," he answered. "Let's start with the most important item we need to talk about…."

Clara's breathing stopped as he took her arm to spin her to look at him.

"You're staying at the cottage," Jason added. "I've slept on that couch out of laziness more times than I care to admit. It's mine tonight. That's a done deal."

Clara felt a release of anxiety with his comment until a touch of disappointment appeared. Logically she knew with his girls in the house, and Callie in the picture, he was not going to do anything to advance a relationship with her. And, given it would have been the first time she would have had to make that level of decision in over twenty years, she was thankful to be putting it off for when the girls were hopefully not there. The lingering fear, however, was that the opportunity to be with Jason was dying. And, without realizing it, they were already turned and heading back to the cottage.

"The other thing is to ask you why you're here."

The question was the one that she expected. It would have been easier had she called in advance to offer to bring the car and Zoe back to him. Zoe's uneasiness gave the perfect reason. But, the element of surprise intrigued her to see how he would react. To call in advance would make it transactional. At best, a friend doing something for a friend. At worst, an employee doing something for her boss. She wanted it to be a surprise gesture of her own doing. His reaction would be tell-tale to his interest in them. Clara started to speak then stopped out of frustration and to frame her words perfectly.

"Do you believe in God, Jason?"

The question she used to answer his questioned mystified him. He stopped to think.

"I think," he paused. "I think I'm what Match.com calls *spiritual, but not religious*."

Jason smiled knowing his answer conveyed at least his look into internet dating after his divorce. Clara held her response. She squinted her eyes to pull more from him.

"I also think," he added. "No, I have FAITH that there was a creator. I mean, look around at all of this and think about everything you know. It's the perfect living system. Something, at some time, created all of this. It's so perfect yet so messed up at times. My personal feeling is that whoever created this wonderful garden of life has either gone on vacation or is letting it fend for itself."

"So, in other words," Clara clarified, "God's plan for you, as well as for me, is to just let things happen?"

"It sure seems that way. Why did you ask me that?"

"Because, I was married to the love of my life who was the man no other man could ever have pulled me from. We shared the same love of life, the same aspirations, and the same faith in God. And despite all of that, and against all the odds that we should meet, we found each other and started an amazing life together. THEN... IN A BLINK... he was dead.... the farm was heading into foreclosure... and you show up."

"Well, I'm glad to be here for you. It, rather it with you, is an exceptionally good investment."

"Jason, you're not getting what I'm saying," Clara inserted into his platitudes. "Is it possible that God brought us together to be more than business partners?"

With that question, the conversation Jason wanted to navigate carefully just got blown out of the water. He never considered divine intervention beyond anything more than Callie not finding him at soccer fields when she went looking for him when his kids were in tournaments near her home. If God had a plan for him and Clara, then why was Callie back in the picture in such a dire situation?

"I felt this coming," Jason admitted as he ran his fingers through his hair. "If I'm being honest with you, I've felt it too. You're exactly who I'd be looking for if I was looking for someone."

Clara stayed silent as she watched him struggle. There was more coming that she wanted to hear. But he was stuck and just staring off into the darkness.

"I realize, at best, I'm second," she struggled to say. "I just couldn't let things continue to unfold without sharing my feelings. I really want to share my life with someone special."

Clara started to tear as she trembled. Jason's immediate response was to hug her for comfort as she vented her need and desire to change from widow to being alive again. As her head nested on his shoulder, he cradled it in his hand. Her crying was quiet and peaceful. He could feel the pressure release from her body as calm set in.

As she settled, Clara stepped back unable to look at him. She wiped her tears away with her hands as she nervously laughed. After a quick glance, she looked down, then back up to find his reaction.

"I'm not prioritizing anyone for anything," Jason said slowly.

"Could it be…. that God just has a sick sense of humor and does this to amuse himself?" Clara asked.

"I don't know what to say to that. With Callie and you timing together… maybe?"

The two began to walk again in silence as each thought through the implications of what was being said along with wondering what the other was thinking. As they approached the stairs to the cottage, Jason took Clara's arm to stop her.

"Why did you come here? You could have driven to Williamsburg instead for the handoff. What if I wasn't here?"

"Someone told me recently that the best way to market something is to put it in a place where it stands out, gets noticed, and is wanted. Callie, with her mom's problems, would have been your number one focus there. That level of caring you have for her is what, I think, we both love about you."

Jason watched her eyes soften as she spoke. The word 'love' struck him for its true emotional meaning instead of just a verb to express a real appreciation for a quality he had.

"And," she added while showing a sinister smirk. "I am also conniving... BUT, not insensitive to what she's going through."

Jason smiled to the humor. Clara was positioning for what she wanted. But conniving was never an adjective he would apply to her. Still, one thing lingered that needed answered.

"But how'd you'd know I'd be here?"

Clara studied his face as she paused to answer the question. To tell the truth would be to admit that she had no idea where Jason would be when she arrived. Her hope was that he would be home at the beach. But in hindsight, she should have expected he would still be in Williamsburg with Callie.

Jason began to smile as time ticked away with no answer.

"What are you smiling about?"

"You," Jason replied. "You are really quite beautiful when you're flustered... AND MAD, like you were in the pond."

Clara face illuminated as his confession finished. Her expectations were proving right increasing her confidence to be honest with him.

"Do you want to know how I knew you'd be here?" she asked while closing the space between them.

Jason became anxious as Clara body and face came within inches of his.

"Devine inspiration, Jason. Divine inspiration."

Jason smiled as he considered correcting her word choice.

"I think you mean divine intervention."

"No," she answered while gaining confidence to lean closer. "Intervention is what put us in the same place at the same time with something to solve together. Inspiration is to intuitively know the right place.... and, to have the courage.... to do this..."

As Clara finished her thought, she took his two hands into hers then closed the gap completely to kiss him. Jason held his ground and accepted her touch without either resistance or withdraw. The press of her body and the softness of her breasts on his released endorphins throughout his body. Her lips quivered as they held contact with his. As nervous as Jason was to jump back into the game with any women, Clara was more nervous. The thought of making a move on anyone, particularly her boss, scared her. Being naked in front of and making love to any other man but Tom took that fear to a much higher level. Jason Cartwright was the first man she wanted since the death of her husband. It felt right, strange, and sometimes wrong. As they separated, Jason wet his lips to taste the residue of hers. He felt relaxed and whole while finding Clara standing nervously in front of him.

Satisfied she had made her point and wanting to leave him to think about her proposition, Clara took her exit and started up the stairs as he stood and watched. The fact that Clara just executed the perfect place, see, and want tactic on him made her exponentially more attractive. That tactic was how he made his fortune enabling him to buy Fox Farm. But outside of Callie, with whom he was comfortable having had a loving relationship long ago, he was dealing with the same new prospective lover concerns that Clara was fighting.

21

Maya remained in the house to wait for their return. It was an unexpected change in plan when Rachel, Faith, and Elyse left her behind to go get ice cream. As they approached the cottage, Jason yielded the way to Clara as he slid the glass door open.

"Dad, you need to look at your phone."

Jason stopped and gave a puzzled look. His mind immediately went to Callie and Carolyn. He remembered putting his phone down with his keys on the railing when he arrived and was greeted by Zoe.

"What's wrong?" he asked.

Maya handed him the phone having seen and knowing the urgency of the message. Jason walked to the corner of the living room before activating the screen.

Mom passed away around 9 to be with Dad and God. I'm fine. C.

Jason's heart broke with the news. His eyes welled with tears that he immediately wiped away. He stood silently facing the corner as he gathered his composure, thoughts, and words.

"Callie's mother passed away."

Clara looked to Maya who gave an affirming nod. The text arrived as the girls were heading out to give their dad some space and privacy with Clara. The phone was brought in with his keys to not be forgotten in the darkness. Maya saw the text repeat and knew she had to stay. It was not news to receive during a casual text check.

Jason looked at the time of the text which was just before 9PM.

He then looked at the current time which was after eleven. Two hours had passed since she texted. He wondered how she was doing. He was afraid of the amount of time that had passed without a response. Without hesitation, he went outside, to their bench, to call her.

"Jason," Callie answered with a groggy voice.

"Cal, I'm so sorry," he replied. "Are you OK? Is everyone OK?"

"We're fine. We got home about thirty minutes ago."

"I'm sorry sweetie. I was on the beach."

"It's OK. I'm good," she answered. Her slight gasping revealed she was crying.

"Do you want me to come up there?"

"No. It's OK. I'm good," she repeated, still gasping.

Callie's quiet exhaustion and answers suggested that she had sedated herself. Whether by alcohol or something else, she was fading off which was a good thing for her to do now to handle the loss of her mother.

"Callie?" Jason asked to see if she was still there. The line stayed live; but Callie was gone.

# # # #

Years before Callie's father died, he and Carolyn had made their funeral and burial arrangements in advance. The details were planned down to the hymns to be sung, the readings, and who the pallbearers were to be depending upon when each passing happened. The age of the male grandchildren made selecting or not using any of them a contingency.

The original six pallbearers were to be Callie's sons Michael and Will, Patty's husband Brian, Maggie's husband and adult son, and Chase. The plans that were in place were never either thought of or updated when the divorce launched. Just after Carolyn passed away, Chase immediately contacted Michael in Spain to be on a plane home the next day.

Carolyn's long desire, that she repeated many times, was that she never wanted to be a bother to her children. Her funeral arrangements were designed with that in mind. Had her death not been sudden, she would have stressed over and changed pallbearer number six from Chase to a contingent free-agent to be named later.

Jason's follow-up call the next morning gave him comfort that Callie was in a good place mentally and had the support of her family around her. Carolyn's death ended all conversation between Jason and Clara about the what-ifs of their cosmically aligned meeting and relationship. After ending his call with Callie, Jason sat alone, in the dark, on the bench overlooking the ocean. Clara waited a few hours then went to bed. When she and Maya walked out of the house to go rent the car, Jason was swimming beyond the waves with his white floating bullet in tow. Clara left a brief note without saying good-bye.

Chase continued to stay at Carolyn's house which added to the awkward situation as more grandchildren arrived to take bunk space in the basement. Chase pitched the idea that he could sleep with Callie as he always did after they married and up until the night he moved out. Callie did not share that need and rejected his proposition fearful it would excite unwanted friction between him and Jason at a time when peace was needed.

Carolyn's plan stipulated that her funeral was to occur two days after her death. The funeral home and church were both able to accommodate the schedule. There were no suspicious surroundings to her passing. And, there was time to properly prepare the gravesite for burial.

When Jason offered to drive to Williamsburg and stay in a hotel, Callie declined. She was heartbroken and wanted time alone to prepare for the service and burial. Her sisters were with her for comfort. Her children were all there too. She never mentioned Chase. Jason understood his presence anywhere near the house with Chase still there would create unneeded stress on the entire family. He knew it was best for them that he stay away.

# # # #

The funeral was scheduled to start at 11AM. The first run of Carolyn's obituary ran the morning of the service. It read like a story starting with her childhood in Grosse Pointe Farms outside of Detroit followed by her boarding school years at Miss Porter's in New England. Her story expanded to Smith College where she met Callie's dad who was two years ahead of her at Yale. They married before she graduated then moved to Pittsburgh for her dad to attend law school and where he spent his career as corporate legal counsel. The survivor list included each daughter, noting spouses in parenthesis, along with an oldest to youngest listing of each grandchild. It bothered Jason that Chase was still listed as Callie's spouse.

Despite the beautiful weather, Jason abandoned his daily swim to have time to dress and be ready to roll by 8:30AM. Fully prepared to attend Carolyn's service either by himself or by Callie, he was surprised when his four girls appeared dressed and ready to go with him. They decided to take two cars to enable them to return while he stayed.

The two-hour drive to Williamsburg was without incident and seemed fast. The GPS predicted their arrival at 10:15AM giving them time in case something along the way happened to slow them down. The prediction, however, was five minutes aggressive. They arrived at 10:20 to a parking lot already filling with cars. A procession of family vehicles behind a hearse was parked at the bottom of the stairs near the front of the church. Jason, with Rachel and Faith riding, parked the Volvo in an open parking slot. Maya, driving with Elyse, parked the Mini next to them.

The church and property around it felt perfect for Callie's family. As Jason scanned the procession line, he saw Callie's Range

Rover parked behind Patty's Mercedes near the hearse. He felt hope when Chase's Maserati was not in the procession.

Up the stairs from the hearse, there was a large, oak, double door facing the road that was propped open. After working a plan full of if-then contingencies, Jason walked in to find Callie while the girls waited outside. Their fail-safe was that he would find them before the service started unless Callie needed him.

Jason walked into the sanctuary slowly noting its beautiful and massive stone construction. Elegant stain-glassed windows adorned three of the four walls filtering soft light onto the parishioners. The church capacity was large. But the gathering was small filled mostly with older friends from the community.

"Jason," whispered a voice from a pew.

As he turned, he saw the face of his childhood friend Sandy Worth. Sandy was Callie's good friend from her Pittsburgh childhood and his best friend's younger sister. Sandy was the reconnection catalyst for Jason and Callie after they first met in a buffet line when Callie was seventeen and he was twenty-two. Callie adamantly denied that having ever happened. Jason said it was the moment he fell in love with her.

"Sandy, hey," Jason whispered back as she side-stepped through the pew to greet him. "Where's Callie?"

Sandy smiled as she slid to him then pointed to an alcove room by the back of the church. Jason gave her a soft hug and promise to talk later. She smiled as she looked at him then patted him on the chest as he turned to go look for her.

The door to the alcove was a thick, planked, oak construction with a small stained glass window in the middle. As Jason arrived to look for Callie, Patty grabbed his arm from behind.

"I need a favor," she said. "We're short a pallbearer. Chase is out. You're in."

Patty's resolute tone and directive amused him.

"It would be my honor," he replied softly before getting an appreciative hug in response.

"Thank you, mom actually asked after you visited," Patty whispered. "Welcome back to the family."

Patty patted him on the chest as she smiled then handed him a boutonniere for his lapel. She then led him into the alcove to find Callie with her three kids and Chase.

Chase was first to notice Jason's arrival and made no effort to hide his look of displeasure. In return, Jason stopped and waited until Callie looked up to invite him over.

"I'm so very sorry, Cal," he said as he awkwardly navigated through her boys to give her a hug.

"I see Patty asked you," Callie said, eyeing the boutonniere in his hand.

"Of course," Jason replied. "It's my honor."

Jason stepped back to create space between him and Callie. He had a keen awareness of being unwelcome by at least two of the five members of her family.

"This is my oldest son, Michael," she said directing her hand toward him.

Jason smiled as the twenty-four-year-old man that stood a few inches taller, and likely ten inches leaner in the beltline to his dad, repositioned for the introduction. Jason extended his hand to greet Callie's oldest son. Michael looked at it then back at Jason with no interest to reciprocate.

"Michael!" Callie whispered sternly.

"It's OK. I understand," Jason replied while withdrawing his hand. "I'm sorry."

Chase watched the interaction without comment content that the son who had not spoken to him was also rejecting Jason. Callie helped Jason place the boutonniere in his lapel. She stepped back to admire the finished product.

"My mom would be delighted," she smiled with tears glistening in her eyes. "She asked for you."

Chase's fist clenched on the combined sight and comment. His twenty-five years to Jason's zero just got slammed in front of his children.

The pallbearers were called to start the procession to escort the casket into the church. The rest of the family followed. Chase joined Callie and Lizzie in the family section. Jason was intrigued that Chase was being permitted the honor of still being family. But Callie's family was strong on appearances; and their divorce was not yet final.

The service was gloriously fitting to the nature of Carolyn. The hymns were supported by a small choir ensemble. A soloist sang *The Lord's Prayer* and brought tears of joy to everyone. Jason's sightline included Callie seated with Chase beside her and Lizzie next to him. He participated in all the rituals in sync with her. He took communion behind her to confirm his belief that Jesus died for his sins. As Jason watched Chase go through the motions, he felt Chase should have exhausted all of God's forgiveness by now.

As a non-Catholic, Jason received a blessing from the priest instead of the traditional wafer and wine. He understood the importance to recognize the different symbolisms between Catholicism and his Presbyterian upbringing. He regretted it ever being a friction point with Callie when they attended a church-required retreat that added to his pre-marital anxiety. She was willing to sign a commitment to raise their children Catholic when they had previously discussed other denominations somewhere in between. Jason's current practice of *spiritual but not religious* made him realize that raising the kids Catholic should never have been an issue.

Callie insisted she be part of the service to celebrate her mother's life and struggled through a reading her mother had chosen for her to read. Psalms 27:1-4's summarized meaning was *With God by your side, you can make it through this dark valley*. Her emotions flared as she read through the words. Once completed, she had difficulty returning to her pew. Chase met her halfway down the altar stairs and held her arm until she was seated next to him again. She dissolved into sobbing while being held by him in the moments that followed.

Maggie and Patty joined as a pair to deliver a warm, hearty, and humorous recollection of their mother, their parents, and their times as a family. Jason watched Callie rebound with the laughter that came with the stories taking a moment, now and then, to wipe tears that continued to flow. Jason thought about his conversation with Clara and the reality of God. In Callie's face, he saw a faith that believed. She was now accepting her mother was with God and by her dad's side again.

As the service ended, Jason stood to join the other pallbearers to deliver Carolyn's casket and body out of the sanctuary to its final resting place on the hill. As he grasped the handle on the side of the casket, he looked straight ahead to find Callie in his peripheral vision standing with Chase at her side. Her eyes showed red as she caught periodic tears with a tissue in her hand. As the music started, Jason walked in step with the five other pallbearers to the waiting hearse that would deliver Carolyn to be with Callie's dad.

Rachel, Elyse, Faith and Maya had no instructions for what to do after the service. As their dad assisted the loading of the hearse, they went to the Mini to wait. Jason pointed for them to pull behind to follow the procession that was going to drive less than half of a mile to Carolyn's gravesite. Patty's husband Brian invited Jason to ride with them as Chase retook command of Callie's Range Rover.

As some parishioners and family gathered near the gravesite, the six pallbearers appeared carrying the heavy casket up the hill. From Jason's experience, the effort was always daunting for six able men on a flat run. The inclusion of young men in the middle of the six added burden to him being on one of the four corners. They finished the journey just as Jason was about to break a sweat. After placing the casket on the lift above the grave, each man rejoined his family for final prayers.

Callie and Chase along with her sisters and their spouses sat in a row of chairs by the casket. Their children stood behind their parents. Carolyn's church community and their friends huddled behind in support. Jason's daughters, feeling out of place, lingered to the side. He joined them there for the final acts of the service.

As each member of the family said their final goodbye with a flower and palm print on the casket, Jason watched Callie say her goodbye with an extended touch on the mahogany. Chase placed his own flower with hers then quickly placed his hand print over Callie's in an apparent declaration of rights to his wife. Jason looked away as the procession of family continued. After the final prayer, Jason walked back to the Mini with his girls to give them permission and directions to leave.

Jason expected that his permission to go would get his girls quickly mounted-up and on their way back to the beach. Each, however, expressed a desire to give their condolences to Callie and her family before they left.

Callie separated from Chase and her children when she reached the road instructing them to return to the car. She smiled as she approached Jason showing sincere appreciation that he and his girls were there to celebrate her mom's life. As she arrived, he heard engines start and watched the Range Rover pull away.

"Your ride just left," he said.

"It's ok. I told them to go. We can walk back down. It's a beautiful day."

Callie's eyes still glistened with a surplus of tears. She smiled as she looked at each of his girls then held her arms open as Rachel approached.

"I'm so sorry," Rachel whispered.

The embrace was genuine from both directions as Elyse followed then Faith. As Maya arrived, Callie took a moment to study the face of her kindred spirit. Two youngest daughters will always have a special bond because of the natural decay of parental power they enjoyed. Callie put her hand to Maya's cheek before giving her a firm embrace.

"Thanks so much for coming," she said still clutching Maya as if her own.

"Of course," Maya replied uncertain to why this embrace was so long.

Callie released Maya and stepped back to study them again. Her smile reappeared to appreciate their support knowing that they were anxious to get going. Each daughter squeezed their dad's arm as they headed back to the Mini. As they drove by Jason and Callie, they all waved a final goodbye before turning still to respect the sanctity of the area as they passed back down through the cemetery to the front of the church.

Lizzie, Will, Michael and Chase were gathered by the front stairs looking back to the hillside as the Wolfpack red, convertible Mini with its top down and two white racing stripes on its bonnet passed by. Lizzie watched and waved still jealous of the pack of sisters and the cute car. Each of Jason's girls waved back as they passed. Elyse caught Will's attention with a pointed finger followed by a wink to wish him *better luck next time*. She then looked to the floor to hide her amusement.

As the Mini left the parking lot and began accelerating down the road, the decibel level they had entering Carolyn's driveway days earlier returned prematurely to echo through the valley. Jason rolled his eyes as Callie laughed.

"Life does go on," she said.

The combined sight of the Mini quietly cascading through the cemetery with four heads of hair blowing then off into the distance with music blaring was a welcome comic relief. As Jason returned his attention to Callie, she was clutching something in her hand. A pained smile came to her face as she opened her palm to show him what she was holding.

"You?" she asked.

Jason stared at the flat, coin sized, ball marker with the Three Rivers Golf Club logo, shook his head *yes*, then looked back at Callie.

"I drove by the church when I was driving around. The name sounded familiar. So, I Googled your dad's obituary. When I saw I was right, I stopped in at the office to get directions to his grave. I needed to talk with him. I believe he was listening and agreed."

Callie's eyes welled with tears as she visualized her dad talking to the Jason who was standing in front of her. Her dad loved Jason when they were younger. She knew he would have loved the man he was today. She knew what the topic was. A tear flowed down her cheek.

"I'm glad you two talked."

22

The church bell tower could be seen from every plot in the cemetery. It was a beacon for souls seeking their life beyond. It was also to comfort those who they had left behind. Jason kept his eye on it as he and Callie walked the single lane road back in silence. To cool from the heat, Jason removed his jacket then threw it over his shoulder. The motion brought Callie back to them. She reached to take his hand in hers then squeezed it tightly to secure her hold.

As they continued in silence, Jason looked periodically to check her state of mind. As his eyes would lock on hers, she would force a smile then look away.

"Just say it," he said to give her the nudge.

Her grip tightened as she thought. Her eyes were focused on the road. Jason looked off into the sky to keep his composure and to wait.

"You always know the day will come when you have to say goodbye to the people you love the most," she said then paused.

Jason thought about her words as he continued to look upward. When he shifted back, he saw her look away from him again.

"I buried my dad which I never thought I'd get over. I miss him every single day. But I got over the pain, found life again, and have lived."

Callie's voice whimpered at the end of her comment as her face dropped to toward the pavement.

"I knew my mother wasn't going to outlive me. But it never

seemed possible that she would be gone so suddenly. SHE WASN'T EVEN SICK. She was my rock, Jason. Now, my mom, IS GONE!"

Callie began to cry again. Jason released her hand to hold her close. Her body felt smaller as she struggled through her emotions. He wanted to stop to settle her down. But she kept forging forward. Then, as if a switch flipped, she stopped to face him.

The look on her face brought back the day they first met. Her natural beauty and allure were undeniable. Her look, as she fussed to tug his shirt taut, was warm and loving. The smile that was lighting her face was turning happy.

"You're so fucking handsome, it's killing me," she said with a laugh that pushed through the tears that began to flow again. "Your nice swimmer's body... that salt-n-pepper hair."

As Callie kept her palms on his chest, Jason felt relief in her words and her cavalier use of the f-bomb in a cemetery. But that feeling dissipated when her face turned serious and her eyes locked in on his.

"Jason Cartwright, you are the love of my life," she said as she began to feel her soul bleed out of her body. "But my family IS... MY... LIFE."

Her strong declaration finished with an air of defeat. She took a moment to study him from head to toe then looked away to cry.

"Callie."

"Jason, I can't," she whispered. "I can't destroy my family. Chase and I talked after mom died and most of yesterday. He says he loves me."

Jason's first thought as he watched her cry was *yeah, loves to cheat on you*. But he kept it to himself.

"I also need to be married," Callie added, "and, you don't."

"We can get there," Jason interjected. "I want to be with you."

Callie's eyes closed to his concession. A soft exhale brought her needed tranquility to think.

"I'd always feel like I forced you."

"Cal, if you had just held with me thirty years ago, we'd be married now."

"I'm so sorry," she answered. "I'm sorry to do this to you. I'm sorry to be doing this to me."

"He'll cheat again. People don't change."

The pain in her eyes told him she agreed. But her nature was protective. Callie would do anything to keep her children in her fold to include sacrificing her happiness even as they separate into adulthood. The need to be present as a family at graduations, weddings, births, and christenings was vital to her. Consistency and appearance were more important than happiness.

"My biggest fear," she said, "is that you are right. He'll leave me again; I'll be back in divorce court; and, you'll be gone."

Jason's blank expression held as Callie admitted expecting what he knew was going to happen. During her fall visit, Jason gave Chase the benefit of the doubt by saying he did not know if he was either the greatest guy on earth or a complete douche bag. He found no comfort in learning the answer. Chase will cheat again. The only question in Jason's mind was when he would get caught.

"When I got divorced, I felt dead inside," Jason said softly. "My biggest fear was loneliness. Starting over with a woman I likely had not met yet was a very close second. I thought talking to you was a million to one shot. Getting this far was unthinkable. I honestly felt that God was intervening for us."

The confession he was making troubled Callie. She knew the unbelievable effort and investment he made to position himself to be found by her. Having that come together in a short timeframe had the fingerprints of a higher being pushing them back together. Jason paused as he thought of one final point he wanted to make. But he knew it would have a cost.

"When I saw you last fall at the gas station, my breathing stopped. I got that tingly feeling that you get when you look across the room to see the one you love more than anything else. And when you left with him, it crushed me more than you can imagine. But I had a glimmer of hope then that you'd be back."

Callie smiled at his faith in their destiny to be together. But her belief was that her marriage would survive her lifetime. Their opportunity to be together died with that decision. Her heart was breaking for him.

"This time," he said, "I don't have that same feeling. I don't believe I will ever see you again."

Callie gasped as he verbalized his expectation. She felt her cheek quiver as her eyes and sinuses welled with pressure. The reality that she was letting him go was finally real to her. Jason was giving her opportunity to give hope for a future together. But he was also finally ready to close the door on them to move on. The pain in that thought was crippling.

"I never thought there'd be anyone but you," he added.

"Maybe finding each other last year and again this summer was to free us from each other?"

Jason pressed his lips together hard to keep from crying. His dream was ending. His *ONE* was saying goodbye forever.

"No," he muttered. "I don't want that. I want you. I want us. I know that is our destiny. But I honestly can't keep doing this…"

Callie eyes exploded with tears as she watched Jason crumble. The torture to release his hope to be with her was shattering his being. She took his hand in hers and squeezed them lightly. She wanted to kiss him.

"My family is evaporating in front of me, Jason," she sobbed. "I can't handle that."

Callie would remember later that she made the same statement to Carolyn less than a year ago before deciding to check-out Jason *from afar*. The discussion at that time was the loss of her dad and her three kids heading into adulthood. Carolyn's response talked about life's evolution as time passes to present new, equally important life focuses. That change was inevitable.

"You are the love of my life," Jason whispered as his eyes met hers. "I would die for you which would be so much easier than this is because I have to now go on knowing you're out there, accessible, and living with some fucking asshole who does... not... deserve... you."

"Knowing you're out there too will haunt me too," she answered. "I just have no other choice."

23

Patty emerged out the church's front door to find Callie and Jason approaching slowly, hand-in-hand as they finished their walk from the gravesite. Chase and her children were still waiting for her return at the foot of the stairs.

The sidewalk from the cemetery road cut the corner and led to the top of the stairs by the door. Patty could see on their faces that more than just her mother had been laid to rest that day. Callie's face and eyes were puffy. Jason was working hard to not make eye contact.

"I was going to send out a search party for you two," Patty joked as they arrived.

Jason looked to Callie who remained silent. Struggling to hold his emotions, Jason looked to Patty with bloodshot eyes and a forced smile.

"I'm so sorry," she said noticeably deflated by her revelation.

"Me too," Jason said as he gave her a hug good-bye. "I'm going to get going."

Patty nodded as he backed away. She put her hand on his sleeve for comfort. Jason forced a second smile to acknowledge her kindness.

"Cal, I'm going to go," he said as he faced her. "Be careful."

Callie's smile showed regret and fear. There was a glimmer in her eyes that said she wanted to change her mind. But her rigid body was not giving in and was willing to fight all her combined urges to change her mind until he was gone.

"I love you," she said as she hugged him.

"I love you back," he answered. "And, to answer the question you asked last fall... Yes, Callie. I am in love with you. I never fell out of love with you, ever."

Callie's mind drifted to the words as she unconsciously moved to kiss him. As their faces came together, she abruptly diverted the point of their touch from his lips to his cheek. She knew that touch of his skin to hers was to be her last sensual memory of him. As they released, Jason closed his eyes as his hand held hers. His turn away and release of her hand that soon followed were simultaneous. He did not look back as he descended the stairs.

The path back to the car required walking down the stairs and past the landing where Callie's family was still standing. Taking an alternate route would be an act of submission to Chase that was never going to happen. As he reached the bottom of the stairs, Jason looked up to lock eyes with Chase. The dead, empty feeling he had after his divorce had returned. Chase made no attempt to hide a smug look of victory meant to rub in what he already knew. Jason was heading home for good without Callie.

Jason considered ignoring her family to get on his way back to the beach. But his eyes met Lizzies whose innocence and admiration of his daughters, and possibly of him, encouraged him to walk near and touch her shoulder goodbye.

"Thanks for your help today," Chase remarked. "I mean, as pallbearer."

Patty and Callie gasped as they watched Chase make a flippant remark as Jason walked by. The words he said were not heard. But it was clear from his smug expression and Jason's immediate stop that Chase said something arrogant and inappropriate.

"You can still change this," Patty implored.

Jason took a short pause to think about whether a response was warranted. And, if so, what that response should be. As he turned to walk toward Chase, Callie grabbed Patty's arm for support. She could see Chase clench his fists expecting another go of their past fight. She feared for her two sons who began to panic on what was about to unfold.

"You'll cheat on her again." Jason started. "Callie's love and LIFE isn't a competition to WIN. You have no shame. You have NO SOUL. SHE DESERVES TO BE HAPPY. Your FAMILY, deserves to be HAPPY."

Chase maintained his smug expression that did not waiver through Jason's declarations. Jason was conceding defeat. Chase had won and loosened his fists before Jason turned to walk away. As he gleefully looked to his three children, their immense disappointment in him was clear in their eyes. They knew Jason was right. Their dad was not trustworthy. He would cheat again. When Chase looked up for Callie, he found her eyes following Jason to his car as Patty's burned a hole through him.

Callie watched the taillights of the Volvo illuminate as the sound of its engine starting sent a shiver up her spine. Her eyes stayed on him as he pulled forward and turned toward the exit back to the beach and Asheville. She knew from his words and actions that their time was over. Her soul ached to see *the love of her life* leave.

As the Volvo approached the parking lot exit, it stopped. In the rearview mirror, Jason could see Chase and Callie's children watching him from the base of the church stairs. Their bodies stood still as they glared in his direction waiting for his final departure. After waiting a few seconds, Jason turned the wheels to redirect his car back into the hills of the cemetery. He wanted to say a final good-bye and to deliver the apology he still owed Callie's mom and dad.

24

The late afternoon August air at Fox Farm was hot and hung without any breeze. As he pulled through the front gate, Jason saw the familiar dark red Chevy Suburban with Thule luggage box on top and a loaded bike rack hanging off its back. Rebecca's two boys and daughter were next to the pond surveying the fallen tree that Jason tried to remove earlier in the summer. The water level was back to normal meaning that something, somewhere, had given way to allow the natural flow of spring water in and out to resume.

As Jason appeared in view at the front door, he heard Rebecca talking to Clara about the cabin, where it was, and whether Jason had arrived. Clara saw him appear behind Rebecca with his finger on his lips to keep his arrival a surprise. As he touched her shoulder, Rebecca turned with an excited look knowing who it was and happy to see him. Clara smiled as the two friends reunited then watched Zoe jump into the pond to create a splash that sent the geese flying. She then waited anxiously for Callie, who did not appear.

As he stood on the front porch to watch Rebecca's Suburban disappear into the same trees that led back to the *Flying Dutchman*, Jason watched Zoe follow the truck to the driveway then circle back to hassle the geese again on the other side of the pond.

For the past few weeks, Jason took time to finish enjoying the remaining days of vacation with each of his girls at the beach before they headed back to work and to school. He then took some my-time by himself just to think and to enjoy his beach friends again. The salt, the sun, and the sand were a welcome reprieve after losing Callie. But they also quickly ran their course with too many memories of his time there with her. He was ready for a change to some mountain relaxation. His favorite rocking chair was empty. He took a seat to just breath and enjoy the moment.

"Welcome back.... BOSS," Clara said sarcastically as she backed out the front door with two glasses of sweating sweet tea.

Although they had talked a number of times since Clara's visit to *Serenity Now*, their conversations were strictly business. Jason did not volunteer anything regarding Callie; and Clara did not ask. Her desire, and fear, was to not do anything that would ruin their working relationship while also not having her heart broken again.

Jason automatically stood as Clara arrived. He always did when people walked into the room. As she set the teas on the table by the rockers, Clara turned toward him to get the latest on his drive in, his girls, and Callie. The smile and hug he gave her was without warning, unexpected and passionate. Her knees wobbled as his embrace stirred the tingling she was fighting to forget. And for a moment, his breathing stopped.

Made in the USA
Coppell, TX
25 June 2020

29272122R00136